ALSO BY KIRBY LARSON

Novels

Audacity Jones to the Rescue

Audacity Jones Steals the Show

Dash

Duke

Dear America: *The Fences Between Us*

The Friendship Doll

Hattie Big Sky

Hattie Ever After

Picture Books
with Mary Nethery

Nubs: The True Story of a Mutt, a Marine & a Miracle

Two Bobbies: A True Story of Hurricane Katrina, Friendship, and Survival

LIBERTY

KIRBY LARSON

SCHOLASTIC INC.

Copyright © 2016 by Kirby Larson

This book was originally published in hardcover by Scholastic Press in 2016.

This book is a work of fiction. Names, characters, places, and incidents are either the product of the author's imagination or are used fictitiously, and any resemblance to actual persons, living or dead, business establishments, events, or locales is entirely coincidental.

ISBN 978-0-545-84072-9

10 9 8 7 6 5 4 3 2 1   18 19 20 21 22

Printed in the U.S.A.   40

First printing 2018

Book design by Ellen Duda

For Eli, braver than dragons and giants

TABLE OF CONTENTS

CHAPTER ONE

Not My Dog

Thomas Edison said, to invent, you need a good imagination and a pile of junk. Fish Elliott had both. Unfortunately, he also had Olympia. Fish heard her before she even poked her braided head through the loose board in the fence between their yards.

"Aren't you done with that yet?"

Fish grabbed a hammer, pounding extra loud to drown her out.

"It'd go faster if you let me help." She slipped through the narrow opening in the fence. If they had been allowed to attend the same school, that loudmouth in his class would've called her String Bean. Olympia's grandmamma, Miss Zona, said that Olympia had to turn around twice to catch her own shadow.

"It was a pure accident with your model plane," Olympia said, tossing an imaginary pebble and hopscotching across the yard.

That "pure accident" left Fish's B-17 with a broken wing.

He braced one piece of wood against his bad leg, and held another up to it at right angles, tapping a nail to fasten them together. With every tap, though, the pieces of wood slipped apart. After the third try, he threw everything down in frustration.

"Let me help steady those." Olympia reached over. "Now pound."

The nail went right in.

She brushed her palms together, a know-it-all smile on her face. "Looks like you *could* use an extra pair of hands."

Fish grunted, and kept nailing. He tapped two more pieces together and then two more, until the frame was more or less square. Sometimes, there was a goodly distance between what he drew in his plans and what got built. Did Thomas Edison ever have problems like that? Sure as shooting, Andrew Jackson Higgins didn't. Mo's boss was the most famous man in New Orleans — maybe the world. His sister said that even Hitler knew about Mr. Higgins. "He calls him the New Noah," Mo told Fish.

She brought home a different story from work every night. Fish's favorite was when some big brass from the Navy told Mr. Higgins there was no way a small company like Higgins Industries could build ships on assembly lines. Mr. Higgins told that admiral, "Like heck we can't. Just watch me." Only he didn't say "heck." If such words had come out of Fish's mouth, Mo would've cleaned it with a bar of Palmolive.

Olympia tapped Fish's project with the toe of her saddle oxford. "What's it going to be?" she asked.

"You'll see when I'm finished." Fish picked up a hunk of chicken wire.

"A crawfish trap?"

He pointed at the size of the holes in the chicken wire. He'd been in town long enough to learn about crawfish. "They'd climb right out."

"Oh, yeah. Ouch! Danged skeeter!" Olympia used her thumbnail to make an X on a mosquito bite on her arm before slapping it three times. "Well, you must be counting on catching something big," she pressed. "That trap could hold three possums and a couple of squirrels."

Fish hadn't planned on building such a large trap. But Mo wouldn't let him use a saw when she wasn't around. "The bigger it is, the less likely that critter eating your grandmamma's Victory Garden will see it. It's like camouflage."

Olympia wrapped a braid around her finger, her brown eyes challenging him. "You don't say."

"It's my trap." Fish tested the joints to see if the nailing job would hold. "I guess I know what I'm doing."

"I saw Roy's car here again the other night." Olympia started stacking the unused scrap wood into a neat pile. Now Fish would never be able to find anything. "He's awful handsome in that Navy uniform."

She should mind her own beeswax. Roy was okay, but Fish had set three places at their dinner table too many times lately. Roy said Mo's cooking was better than anything he got at the Navy base. Why a lightning bolt hadn't struck him dead for saying that, Fish had no idea. His sister could change the oil in a car, rotate a set of tires, and replace a worn clutch, but cooking edible food seemed beyond her. If Miss Zona hadn't sent over a plate of gumbo or some red beans and rice once in a while, Fish and Mo might have starved to death.

Olympia started humming "Here Comes the Bride" while he wrestled a piece of chicken wire into place. It was hard to imagine that someone so ornery sang solos in her church choir.

"I can manage on my own now." Fish picked up his plans, puzzling over them. How was he going to fasten on the trapdoor?

Olympia fiddled with a bent nail. "Why don't you want my help?"

There was the model, of course. Fish kept his eyes on his plans. He wasn't about to explain to Olympia that the last time he'd made a real friend, it was another kid in the polio ward. Someone like him.

"O-lympia!" Miss Zona hollered out the back door. "Come help me shell these peas."

"Wish I could stay longer." Olympia stood up, brushing off her dress.

Church bells chimed the hour. Fish folded the plans into his pocket. "I've got to go anyway." Mo had asked him to pick up some green beans for supper. That meant three places at the table again. Roy was crazy about green beans.

As he step-clomped to Cali's Market, Fish heard the faint mournful blasts of steamships coming and going. He paused to listen, imagining workers unloading bananas and coffee beans from the holds, then reloading with sugar and such. He'd looked up New Orleans in the encyclopedia before he and his sister left Seattle. The map showed the city sandwiched between the bubble of blue that was Lake Pontchartrain and the snaky path of the Mississippi River. Now that he was here, he got the feeling, what with the lake, the canals, the bayous, and the river, New Orleans was nothing more than a sponge floating in the middle of an enormous bathtub. There was so much water, even the cemeteries were aboveground.

He passed by Campbell's Hardware with the war poster in the window — BRING THEM HOME SOONER/ BUY WAR BONDS — which always reminded him of Pop. He didn't have to enlist, but he did, saying he could make a difference, and besides, Mo and Fish could take care of themselves just fine. But Fish knew he was the real reason Pop joined up.

"All you need is them green beans?" Miss Rose sounded downright disheartened. "We've got a nice sale on soup," she said. "Three cans for a quarter. And only three points each."

Fish promised to ask Mo about the soup as he handed over the money and the ration book and took the packet of beans. A block away from the market, he spied some guys from school throwing rocks at the corner light post. Fish decided to avoid them by taking the long way around. Pritchard Street didn't look much different from his own: rows of shotgun houses on either side of the road, one of them painted the same shade of pink as Miss Zona's. That reminded him about the trap. What was he going to do about the door?

"That your dog?" a gruff voice called out.

Fish kept walking.

"I'm talking to you, boy." The voice got sharper. "That your dog?"

A man wearing suspenders over a dingy undershirt glared at Fish.

"I don't have a —" he began. Then he turned around to catch a skinny cur hound trotting along behind him. She wore white stockings on her two front legs, and a white bib on her chest. The rest of her was a mottled coppery brown. Kind of like that patchwork quilt Miss Zona threw over her living room sofa. The dog cocked her head at Fish, as if asking, *Don't I know you?*

"She's not mine." Fish didn't see a collar. A stray?

"Well, if I catch her around here again, she won't be anybody's dog," the man snapped. "Bound to go after my chickens sooner or later. Scram!" He flapped his arms and hollered at the dog; Fish felt like he was being yelled at, too. He let out his breath when the man stormed off.

Fish whistled softly, patting his leg, and the dog took a few steps toward him. "That's a girl," Fish encouraged. A few more steps. "Come with me, okay?" He could count her ribs. "I'll find you some food."

She froze, a front paw in the air.

The crabby man barreled around the corner of his house, picking up rocks as he ran.

"Don't hurt her!" Fish yelled.

The man clipped the dog on the hindquarters. She yelped, tearing off down the street, a blur of copper and white.

"She comes back around here again, I'm going to shoot her." The man threw one last rock.

Fish scrambled away, as fast as he could with his bad leg.

That dog needed saving.

And it was up to him to do it.

CHAPTER TWO

Somewhere in North Africa

He and Hans had felt like pirate captains, coming upon the deserted camp and the Tommies' rations. Tins of meat and sausages, fruit, and biscuits hastily buried in the sand. They'd shared their bounty with a few of their *Gruppe*, all of them eating like wolves, inhaling the food before the flies got in. Erich could scarcely remember what it was like to eat without batting away flies.

At least the night had passed quietly; he'd slept like a babe with his full belly. For the first time in months, Erich's dreams were not of the war, or of the Afrika Korps, but of home: He and his brother were bookended by their parents at the dining table. Mutti, Vater, and Friedrich lifted their glasses to him, as if toasting some good news. It was not much, that pleasant dream, but precious in its ordinariness. Erich was reluctant to wake, to leave his family, especially his little brother, Friedrich, behind. But his bladder was insistent. As others in the camp began to stir, Erich pulled on his shorts and shirt, checking his boots for scorpions. Almost worse than scorpion bites were the infections from the cactus thorns. But those were finally healing. Things were looking up. In addition to last night's feast, they'd been able to stay put for a few days. Long enough to set up a camp, to dig into the hardpan and pitch the two-man tents. He bunked with Hans, who was not bad, for a Bavarian. At least he didn't snore.

Outside the tent, Erich stretched, smacking his lips. When was the last time he had truly quenched his thirst? How did the Bedouins survive in this miserable desert? It was crawling with enemies: the brutal sun, the flies, the sand-storms. And, of course, the Americans.

He nodded to Oskar, exiting the nearest tent. *"Guten Tag."*

Oskar nodded back, lit a cigarette. Erich continued on to the slit trench they used as a latrine. He relieved himself, then did up his shorts, shivering. It would be beastly hot soon, but the morning air still bullied him with last night's chill. Despite being a decent student, he had been astonished to learn that, in this desert, the temperature could vary forty degrees between day and night. It was a wonder they hadn't all succumbed to pneumonia.

Erich moved away from the latrine trench, his boot crunching against the sandy crust atop the hard stone. He took another step and hesi-tated, aware of a vibration in the bedrock. A vibration that traveled through his worn leather boot soles, up his legs, and straight into his gut.

His head jerked up, eyes scanning the cloud-less sky. B-17 bombers. The Americans!

"Take cover!" He screamed the warning to his comrades. Why he even bothered, he did not know. This miserable stretch of grit and pain was hardly like the thick forests back home that swallowed men with ease. Here, there was nowhere to hide but the few bomb shelters and trenches they'd been able to carve out of this unforgiving rock. But Erich ran anyway. What else was there to do?

"Hans!" His tent mate could sleep through anything. "Take cover!"

Erich did not hear the bomb. He saw it or, rather, saw the pummeling fist of dust and rock and debris it sent skyward. Blown like a matchstick across the sand, he crashed against a Panzer. Dazed, he shook himself. Took inventory. Everything seemed to be in working order. He staggered away from the tank toward the tent he shared with Hans.

It wasn't there.

Now, as he fought to stay on his feet, he had a vague memory of someone – Oskar? – helping him put his boots back on, handing him a canteen of water, offering words of comfort.

The first thing he was truly aware of after the bombing was an officer waving a white flag. Of his comrades throwing their weapons down. Raising their hands.

Erich shook his aching head, trying to make sense of the scene.

A very tall American soldier – with corn silk hair and inexplicably kind eyes – greeted Erich in perfect German: *"Fuer dich, mein junger Freund, der Kreig is vorbei* – For you, my young friend, the war has ended."

By nightfall, Erich and his unit were in a holding camp. Each man was asked to show his Soldbuch, his military identification booklet. Erich had no trouble with the soldier examining his, but Oskar's had been taken. To be kept as a war souvenir, no doubt, as was Erich's father's watch. It was now in the possession of a smug American private who wore it on his arm with six or seven others he had "liberated" from the captured men.

Later, the Americans brought them food — slices of white bread as sweet and soft as cake — and bowls of stew. Each man even got an orange! Erich devoured every bite. He couldn't imagine why he was so hungry at a time like this, but he was. Besides, this meal might be his last.

After eating, they were marched in small groups to tents. Erich stumbled inside and collapsed on the nearest cot, too exhausted to comment on the luxury accommodations. At least they were luxurious in comparison to those he'd enjoyed in Rommel's forces the past several months. He did not even remove his boots. He rolled onto his stomach, feet hanging off the edge of the cot, and fell dead asleep, no sweet dreams of parents, of Friedrich. No dreams at all.

And that was how Erich Berger celebrated his seventeenth birthday.

CHAPTER THREE

With a Side of Spam

"Oh, gosh, I'm so late." Mo tore down the stairs, through the kitchen to the bathroom. She soon emerged, smelling of Shalimar and Pepsodent, mumbling something about Mr. Higgins having her head. "Don't forget to take out the trash!" She grabbed her hat and pocketbook, and was gone.

Fish crunched his breakfast cereal in the now-quiet kitchen, still thinking about the dog. He hoped she'd found a safe place to sleep. He hoped that man hadn't hurt her.

He was almost out the front door on his way to school when he remembered the trash. He step-clomped back through the house to fetch the can from under the sink. Balancing it against his right leg, he hobbled down the back steps. Something rustled in the shrubs by the shed. A cat? Raccoon? Miss Zona's rabbit? Fish approached slowly. The rustling got louder. When he was just paces away, a copper-colored streak flew out. The dog! And here he was with no treat.

"Hey, girl!" He set the trash can down. Patted his leg. She hesitated, shaking. He took one small step. "I won't hurt you."

She sniffed the air in his direction.

He held out his hand. Moved closer.

And she ran. She was out of sight before he could even think to call her again.

Fish couldn't believe he'd missed catching her a second time. But she'd been in his yard, which gave him an idea. An idea he couldn't do anything about until after school. For one brief moment, he considered playing hooky. He didn't even want to think about what Mo would do if he did. It was going to be torture, but he had to go.

Fish had never made it home from school so quickly. He went straight out to the backyard to rummage around in the shed. None of the stuff in it was theirs; it belonged to the renters before them. But those people were long gone. Finders keepers. He didn't know exactly what he was looking for. Sometimes an open mind was the best way to go about finding what you needed. It was like Thomas Edison once told an employee: "There ain't no rules around here! We're trying to accomplish something!"

Hopeful as Fish was to find a solution for the trapdoor, he didn't think that old lard tin or broken rake or torn fishing net would do much good. Or that stack of magazines. No comics, but some *National Geographic*s and *Life*. He set aside the few issues of *Popular Mechanics* for later. A paint-spattered drop cloth hid an old Schwinn and a stack of cigar boxes. Pushing down the memory of his fifth birthday, he reached around the bike to yank out a couple of the cigar boxes. Fish picked up a pair of rusted needle-nose pliers, some snips, and a mallet before dragging all of his treasures out to the yard. He dropped to a sit, bad leg straight out.

"Now what are you making?" Olympia poked her head through the loose board in the fence.

Fish held one of the cigar boxes on his lap, flipping the lid open and closed. He could use hinges to hook the trapdoor on. That was all well and good for opening. But what could he use to trigger the door to shut? He flipped the lid back and forth again.

Olympia was now settled, cross-legged, next to him. "Mo's going to tan your hide if she catches you smoking that trash."

Fish gave her a disgusted look. "I'm not smoking. I'm thinking." He flipped the lid up, down, up, down, up, down as if repeating that action would make an idea fly into his brain.

"Oh." Olympia sat quietly for about ten whole seconds. "What about?"

"You don't want to hear." Fish had been teased too many times at his old school for sharing his inventions.

She leaned forward, bony elbows resting on scabbed knees. "I truly do." Something in her expression reminded Fish of Nurse Meg. And *she'd* been a real good listener.

He flapped the cigar box lid again. "Well, I can figure out how to fasten the door to the trap easy enough, using hinges," he said. "But then how do I get it closed?"

Olympia's thin face scrunched up as she pondered. "Poke at it with a stick when the critter's inside?"

"I need a way to close it if I'm not here." He waggled the lid again. What could pull it closed?

"Some kind of rubber band?" Olympia suggested. "'Course, that's hard to come by with the rationing." She giggled. "Grandmamma's had to make our undies with drawstrings because there's no elastic to be found. Mine came untied at recess last week and 'bout fell to my ankles."

Fish hid his face behind the cigar box. "You're right. It can't be rubber." Only Olympia would bring up something as embarrassing as underwear.

She turned her head sideways. "How about some kind of doohickey?"

"What?"

"You know, like what helps the blinds go up and down." Olympia made a motion as if pulling cords to open a set of venetian blinds.

Fish closed his eyes and tried to visualize the blinds in his bedroom. There had to be some kind of pulley system in the innards to make them go up and down. His eyes sprang open.

"Does Miss Zona have any empty spools of thread?"

"With all the sewing she does?" Olympia rolled her eyes. "She's got a basket full."

"Can you bring me two?" Fish tapped his lips

with his fingers. He was on the verge of a break-through. If he talked too much, the idea might get talked away. Luckily, Olympia didn't pester him with questions. She ran off and was back in a flash.

"Equipment as ordered!" She gave Fish the wooden spools and he handed her two paper clips to straighten.

While she did that, he poked a tiny hole near the top edge of each of the short sides of the cigar box. He threaded a paper clip through the hole in the center of one of the spools, then through one of the holes in the box, twisting the ends together with the pliers. Now the spool was resting on its side on the lip of one of the short sides of the box. "Look through that jar there for two of the smallest eyes you can find," he told Olympia, repeating the threading process on the other side.

"I see what you're doing!" Without being told, Olympia screwed the pointy end of the eyes into either side of the lid.

Fish sat back. "Now I just need some string."

"Hey!" Olympia untied ribbons from two of her braids. "What about these?"

Fish tied one end of each ribbon to each eye and threaded the other end under each of the sideways spools. He handed one loose end to Olympia — she had helped, after all — and took the other himself. "Ready? One, two, three, pull!"

They both gave gentle tugs and, like magic, the lid pulled up and closed.

"We did it!" Olympia jumped up and did a little dance, hopping from one foot to the next.

"I bet Mr. Campbell has what I need to make it work for the trap." Fish struggled to his feet. He couldn't dance around like Olympia, but he felt a grin lapping against his ears. "Then all I need is some meat for bait."

Olympia stopped her prancing. "Don't you mean carrots?"

"Oh, yeah." Fish caught himself. "I guess I was thinking of supper." He patted his stomach. "I'm pretty hungry. Going to head in and get a snack."

Olympia looked at him funny.

"Thanks for your help." Fish meant it.

Olympia gave the ribbon one last gentle tug. "You can keep these for now. But I'll need them back before church on Sunday." She disappeared through the gap in the fence.

Fish took his cigar box model inside and set it on the kitchen counter. He checked the time; he'd better hurry before Mo got home.

He went to his room and shut both doors. No sense taking chances. He traded his chinos for the only pair of shorts he owned. He never wore them outside. He couldn't hide the limp, but he could his ugly leg, stick thin and white as chalk dust.

Fish glanced at the picture of President Roosevelt he'd taped to his wall. Under it, he'd copied words from one of FDR's fireside chats: *There are many ways of going forward but only one way of standing still.* So far, none of Fish's fix-it ideas had really worked. But FDR hadn't given up, even though he had polio, so neither would Fish.

He retrieved his secret weapon from under the bed. It looked like a kids' swing. Fish positioned his right foot on what would be the seat of the swing, gripping the attached lengths of rope in each hand. Then he pushed as hard as he could, trying to straighten his knee. He counted to ten. Then rest and repeat. *Push, hold, count. Push, hold, count. Do. Not. Stop.* If he did this every day, his knee might begin to bend. *Push, hold, count. Push, hold, count.* It hurt like heck, but it would be worth it when Pop came home. Worth it to hear Pop tell complete strangers, "This is my son. A chip off the old block."

Fish grimaced as he counted again. The pain made his stomach clench. He flopped back on the floor, wiping sweat from his face, panting. It felt like he was back in the hospital, one of those times when the therapy had hurt so bad, he couldn't help hollering. Then Nurse Meg came along and told him to think of his favorite place in the world. "Now imagine you're there," she said in her soft voice. It sounded crazy to Fish, but because it was Nurse Meg, he gave it a go. It had worked then. And it worked now. He sat up, gritted his teeth, and counted to ten five more times.

Pop didn't know that Fish had seen the snapshot he'd chosen to pack when he left for the Army. But Fish did. The one from his fifth birthday, riding his new bicycle, a goofy grin on his face. Fish was smiling so big you could see the missing baby teeth on the bottom. He got the hang of bike riding right away, didn't even need training wheels. Mo told him Pop had bragged about it to all the guys at the repair shop. Four months later, Fish was flat on his back in the polio ward. Never got on the birthday bike again. Pop wanted to remember *that* boy. Not the one he had now. Fish would do whatever it took to be the kind of son that his father really wanted.

He heard Mo fumbling with the lock at the front door. He stashed his device and jumped into his chinos, hurrying to the kitchen. His sister came in as he was taking three plates out of the cupboard.

"Hey, kiddo." She ruffled his hair. "Thanks a bunch." She peeked out the back door as she unpinned her hat and hung it on a hook. "Looks like you're making progress on Miss Zona's trap. Thanks for doing that."

"Well, she's been so nice to us and all." Fish avoided Mo's eyes. She didn't have to know the real reason he was working so hard on the trap. He finished setting the table.

"How are things at work?" That question was a surefire way to distract her.

Mo chuckled as she tied on an apron. "Boy howdy, did we get a passel of complaints. I've told you how Mr. Higgins cranks up the public address system for his little pep talks. Well, he went a bit overboard today. The neighbors appreciated his patriotism but not his salty language. One of them even called the police." She shook her head. "But he gets a fire lit under people and that's what matters."

"What's the count?"

Mo kept a tote board in the office, tallying the number of ships Higgins Industries built. Crews worked around the clock to churn out boats as fast as they could.

"We're on track to break a weekly record. Maybe thirty-nine LCVPs and twenty PT boats." Mo tore some iceberg lettuce into a bowl. "That reminds me; I may have to work late tomorrow or the next night. There's a big wrinkle that needs ironing out. You see —"

A rapping at the front door interrupted Mo. She went to answer it and came back with Roy, still in uniform, hat tucked under his arm.

"Seaman Weathers reporting for duty, sir!" Roy saluted Fish before tossing his hat on the hook by Mo's. "What's cooking?"

"Ask my sister," Fish answered. "I can't tell." This Meatless Tuesday concoction didn't look as bad as last week's, a revolting mixture of eggs, Grape-Nuts, Velveeta, and stewed tomatoes.

Roy laughed again. "I meant, what have you been up to?"

"He's been hard at work on that trap for Miss Zona's garden." Mo dropped a blob of grease into the hot skillet. "That is one good kid."

"You don't have to tell me." Roy smiled at Fish.

Fish hid behind the open icebox door, taking his time getting out the milk bottle.

Roy plunked down on a chair. "It's good to be with friends."

"Tough day at class?" Mo held up the percolator, wordlessly asking if Roy wanted some coffee. He nodded.

"That McDerby is going to be the death of me. Docked me ten points for penmanship on my exam." Roy shook his head. "I'm here to learn to drive a Higgins boat. Not for finishing school. Penmanship! He nearly canceled my Friday night pass because of it."

Mo made a sympathetic face as she set plates of food on the table. "I know he's tough, but there's no one who knows those LCVPs better than Captain McDerby. Even Mr. Higgins says so."

"Well, he thinks the rest of us are dumb as stumps." Roy forked up some green beans. "I'm so glad it's almost over." He buttered a slice of bread, eating it in two bites. "Boy, hon, this is delicious, but I'm starved. You couldn't spare a slice of Spam, could you?"

"Can I have one, too?" Fish piped up.

"It's 'may I?'" Mo made a face. "I take it you boys did not enjoy my crispy baked eggs." She shook her head. "And here I am, trying to be patriotic."

"Nothing more patriotic than feeding a hungry sailor!" Roy held up his empty plate, making puppy dog eyes. Fish followed suit.

Mo laughed as she opened a can, cutting them each a slice. Roy gobbled his down; cold Spam was not Fish's favorite. But he needed it.

"I can't wait for your graduation party," Mo said. "I've heard about it at the office so many times." Her eyes got all dreamy and far away. "The Blue Room at the Roosevelt Hotel! Dinner! Dancing! Imagine. I only hope my dress will pass muster."

Fish pulled his napkin onto his lap, hoping neither of them noticed that it was hiding the slice of Spam.

"Even in coveralls, you'd be the prettiest girl there," Roy said.

"May I be excused?" Fish wanted to vamoose before the mushy stuff.

"What about those green beans?" Mo pointed at his plate. "There are starving children in China, remember."

"Aw, let the kid alone." Roy reached over and stabbed a forkful of Fish's green beans. "I hated vegetables when I was your age, too."

"Now may I be excused?" Fish asked again.

Mo sighed. "I suppose."

"Hey, before you take off. You two busy a week from Sunday?" Roy looked at Fish and then at Mo, who shook her head. "Well, you are now. There's a big war bond sale at Pontchartrain Beach. You can try on gas masks, get free seeds for a Victory Garden, and yours truly will be giving civilians rides in an LCVP." He kind of puffed out his chest.

"Sounds fun, doesn't it, Fish?" Mo poured herself another cup of coffee.

"Sounds swell." It did, but he needed to get going. Fish picked up his plate and set it in the sink. It was his turn to wash, but he'd do that later.

For now, he was going to take a walk around the block. After he grabbed a piece of rope from out back. He patted the wrapped-up Spam in his pocket.

His dog was probably hungry.

CHAPTER FOUR

IIIIIIIIIIIIIIIIIIIIIIIIIIIIIIIIIIIIIIIIIIIIIIIIIIIIIIIIIIIIIII

Near Algiers

The Americans turned them over to the French, who seemed determined to make life as miserable as possible. The Frogs had charming ideas, which included hours of standing at attention in the hot sun, miserable food, disrupted sleep. All meant to crush Erich and his fellow soldiers. Punish them. And from what he had learned of the Fuhrer's actions, Erich couldn't really blame them. Yet, he had not done those awful things. He hadn't even wanted to be a soldier.

Being the youngest of the prisoners granted Erich no privileges. He was regularly questioned by the commanding officer – perhaps they thought because he was the youngest, he'd be the weakest. That showed how little they knew of him. The Tommies had tried psychology on him, but it didn't work. There had not been any rough stuff, but when would his interrogators tire of Erich answering all of their questions with "I don't know"?

Almost the only time Erich spoke now was to his interrogators. He was determined to keep himself to himself. He had heard rumors that the Nazis still had connections, even from the camps. If he said the wrong thing, who knew how that might harm his loved ones? Best to stay silent.

Not a moment went by that he didn't wonder how his family was faring. It had been so long since he'd heard from any of them. Even now, if he thought for one instant about his brother, it was worse than any punishment the French could dream up. Friedrich was so sensitive, so kind, so trusting. Because of his leg, the family had protected him. Erich had protected him. His brother had not learned to be hard, as Erich had been forced to. How would someone like Friedrich survive this war?

To calm himself, Erich turned his thoughts to his grandfather. A big bear of a man who loved nothing more than to stroll through the woods, seeking out fallen limbs. He would cut them into various lengths and then select one piece, studying it. "What do you think is hiding inside, Erich?" he would ask. And Erich would answer: A fox. A wood duck. An osprey. Perhaps even a turtle. Grandfather would hold an impossibly small knife in his huge hands, nicking here, notching there. In an afternoon's time, he would release the requested creature from that stick of wood.

Here, in this camp, Erich felt much like the dead limbs Grandfather collected. And he was going to do whatever it took to stay concealed, to stay hidden. He could not let anyone see the Erich within.

It was his only chance of surviving.

CHAPTER FIVE

Freedom for Liberty

The air smelled of coffee and some kind of perfumey flowers. Nearby, someone wailed "Skylark" on a saxophone. From Miss Zona's drifted the notes to "This Little Light of Mine" being plinked out on the piano. Olympia practicing for church.

The sounds pushed him along Fig Street. Rope tossed over his shoulder, Fish step-clomped down the sidewalk even more slowly than usual. He wondered if he'd ever get used to calling it a banquette, like Olympia and Miss Zona did. He liked all the French-sounding words people used here; sometimes New Orleans was one joyful jumble of sound. Not just music like that sax he could hear when he stopped every few paces to whistle for the dog. But the language and the voices, too. As he strained to catch any bark or whine, he caught the cry of the watermelon man: "Watermelon. Red to the rind!" Never heard that in Seattle.

And he'd never been this close to having a dog back home, either. He stopped to whistle again. Waited. No sign of Liberty.

That's what he'd decided to call her. Mostly because she'd been running free when they first met. Once that name popped into his head, he couldn't think of anything else that suited. "Here, girl!" he called, too shy to use her name aloud. A yappy dog pressed its nose against the glass in a house across the street. But it was a fluffy puffball. Not his Liberty.

He walked on. Take a few steps, stop, whistle and call. As long as he was home by dark, Mo wouldn't fuss. He attracted waves from two neighbors he didn't know, but nothing else. And now he'd reached Carrollton. There was nothing to do but head toward Pritchard Street, so at the next corner, he turned right. It gave him the willies, but he knew he should check out the Chicken Man's place.

Maybe Liberty was so hungry that she'd gone back to the chicken coop. He prayed she didn't bother any chickens. Hopefully, the Spam would be enough to tempt her away. He should have brought a bigger piece.

Though all the houses looked alike, it was easy to pick out the Chicken Man's. Just looking at it made Fish flinch. He crossed over, step-clomping with determination. The mailbox in front bore the name LaVache, painted in crooked letters. The name sounded angry, like the man. Fish paused. The chickens were quiet. A good sign. But if Liberty wasn't here, where could she be?

Fish step-clomped his way to the next house, did an about-face, and step-clomped back again. Three more times he paced back and forth in front of the Chicken Man's house. No sign of anything, person or dog. He whistled softly. Waited.

Nothing.

Maybe someone else took her home.

He shook his head, refusing to consider such a thought. Liberty was counting on him. And he wasn't going to let her down. Even if he didn't have the guts to cut through Mr. LaVache's yard to poke around the chicken coops. Plan B. He made a loop around the block, coming up from behind. Instead of another home on the back side of the LaVache house, there was a pint-sized farm with a Victory Garden ten times bigger than Miss Zona's, and several good-sized chicken coops.

Fish rocked back and forth, from good leg to bad, looking for Liberty while keeping an eye out for Mr. LaVache. If he didn't mind pitching rocks at a pesky dog, he probably wouldn't have any problem pelting a pesky kid.

One clumsy step, then another, and soon he was next to the first chicken coop. Still no sign of Liberty. But the chickens — already tucked in for the night — must've sensed him. One coop started clucking and squawking, which started a commotion in the second and third. Over the hen racket, Fish heard the screen door open and slam shut.

"Who's out there?"

Mr. LaVache. With a baseball bat in his hands. "I hear you, you chicken thief!" He stomped down the steps, stumbling out of his house slippers. He hollered again while he fumbled back into them. "Don't think you can get away!"

Fish scrambled backward as fast as he could. He step-clomped toward a hedge he thought he could hide behind, too scared to notice the tree root snaking its way through the banquette. He went flying, landing hard on the concrete. Gasping for breath, he lay there, unable to get up.

A painful turn of the head revealed Mr. LaVache checking out the chicken coops. Evidently, he'd given up the chase.

After a second, Fish pressed his palms to the banquette and pushed to an awkward kneel, resting on his good knee while the other stuck out stiffly. At least no one had seen him fall. That would mean teasing. Or worse: pity. He pushed back memories of other falls. Too many other falls. Stupid leg.

Something cool tickled his left ear. Fish batted at it and felt a wet tongue. He turned.

"Liberty!" He threw his arms around her, not even minding her smell. He plopped onto his rear and she clambered onto his lap. Her head and forelegs didn't fit, but she didn't seem to mind, intently nosing Fish's pocket. He pulled out the Spam, breaking it into chunks. She inhaled each bite.

"You're still hungry, aren't you?" Fish stroked her bony back. "Come with me. I'll get you plenty to eat." He slowly stood up, holding out the last bit of Spam. "Want this?" The rope had gone flying when he fell. He had to coax her closer.

She licked at the meat, then tried to pry it out of his fingers. With her teeth, but so gently.

"You wouldn't hurt a fly, would you?" He patted her head. "Or Mr. LaVache's chickens." He kept talking, softly, holding the food just out of Liberty's reach. He took a few step-clomps. She followed. A few more. The rope was now inches away.

A pair of bicycles came barreling up the street. Wally and another boy from their school were shouting war whoops and waving their free arms like they were in some Tom Mix western movie.

At the racket, Liberty bolted, leaving the last of the Spam behind.

The other boys stood, pedaling hard, chasing Liberty as she ran. Fish hobbled after them, but he couldn't keep up. Could never keep up.

The chunk of Spam felt slimy in his hand. He pitched it away as hard as he could.

"What's going on?" Olympia trotted toward him. "Those boys going to hurt that dog?"

That thought hadn't even entered Fish's mind. "Go away." Fish began limping home. Olympia walked, too, matching her pace to his.

"So is that why you wanted meat for the trap?" She played with the ribbon around one of her braids. "To catch a dog? That dog?"

Heavy sigh. "Yeah." Fish could've been carrying one of Mr. Higgins's boats on his back, he felt that weighed down by failure. He braced himself for Olympia to confirm it.

Olympia cocked her head, eyeballed Fish. "That's a great idea."

Fish glanced at her. "You think so?"

"Looked like she was about starving. She needs taking care of." Olympia chewed on the hair ribbon. "She come to you?"

Fish nodded, holding out his now empty hands. "I fed her some of my dinner."

Braids bounced. "Well, that's real good. She knows you'll have food. And she trusts you." Olympia tugged on Fish's arm. "Come on. Let's get home and finish that trap. We've got a dog to catch." She picked up the pace. Fish bounced along, trying to keep up.

His steps felt lighter. So did his heart. It felt good to have someone on his side.

Even if it was Olympia.

CHAPTER SIX

Young Mr. Edison

Fish tossed the mail on the table, mostly bills. But a letter from Pop tumbled out. Addressed just to him! He tore it open and read.

> Dear Fish,
> Uncle Sam put me to work on Bailey bridges. It's a lot like working in the garage, taking car engines apart and putting them back together. The motto of our unit is "Forward" because we go ahead of the troops, building bridges, so soldiers and tanks can move to where they're needed. Anywho, I thought you'd get a kick out of knowing that. Mind your sister.
> Pop

It was the first letter Pop had written just to him. Fish read it several more times. He sniffed the paper to see if he could pick up Pop's scent of

Barbasol, engine grease, and Prince Albert tobacco. But the only thing he smelled was paper.

As he put the letter away, the house seemed quieter, lonelier. Fish would give anything to hear Pop's gravelly voice. He hoped he was taking care. Hoped it wouldn't be too much longer before he came home.

Fish shook his head. What had come over him? He was being downright sappy. Maybe it was because he knew Mo would be working late tonight; he wouldn't have anyone to talk to.

He pulled open the icebox, looking for a snack. First thing he saw was the leftover liver curry that Mo said he could have for supper again. Fish could barely gag it down the first time she'd served it. He didn't think it'd be improved, left over. Despite his sister's good intentions, Fish's dinner plans revolved around a peanut butter and jelly sandwich. But there was something that liver curry was good for.

Holding his breath, Fish carried the dish out to the backyard. The pie tin in the trap still had the macaroni and cheese from the night before. He dumped that into the trash, and re-baited it with some of the curry. He waved his hand in front of his face. It sure smelled like something a dog would like.

A head poked through the fence. "Any luck yet?" The rest of Olympia squeezed through. "Whoo-wee! What is that?" She pinched her nose with her fingers.

Fish pointed at the trap. "Mo's liver curry."

"She made you eat that?" Olympia's eyes bugged out.

"She tried." Fish shuddered to remember. "Trust me, no amount of ketchup helped it go down."

"I hear you." Olympia stayed far away from the trap, pulling a jump rope from her skirt pocket. "So did the dog come by?"

Fish hadn't told her about naming Liberty yet. He sighed. "The food hadn't been touched."

"Well, you think you could spare the trap for one night?" She turned the rope, jumping in place. "That durned rabbit's 'bout gobbled up all Grandmamma's bean starts."

"Sure. Tomorrow?" Since it was Miss Zona who had inspired him to build the trap, Fish guessed it was only fair that he actually put it to use in her garden. "We'll use different bait."

"I sure hope so." Olympia started doing some fancy moves, like scissors and front cross. Each landing sent up a puff of dust. "Want to go look for the dog again?"

After school, they had scouted the neighborhood, circling each block carefully, whistling and calling. Olympia even walked Pritchard Street with him, past Mr. LaVache's. When they'd seen him leave in that rattletrap truck of his, Olympia marched right into his yard, peering under shrubs and behind piles of trash, calling, "Here, girl, here, dog!" They spotted no sign of Liberty but met many of their neighbors. Fish's favorites were the Beasley sisters, who dressed like twins even though they weren't and offered him and Olympia fresh-made pralines.

"We've been saving our sugar up for an occasion," said the one Miss Beasley. "We just didn't know what it was going to be. And here it is, making your acquaintances!"

They met Mr. and Mrs. DeSoto — he lost an arm in a traffic accident. No one would hire him but Mr. Higgins. Mrs. DeSoto told them that her husband now worked in the electrical shop at the City Park Plant. Fish felt proud of the man his sister worked for.

That afternoon, they met more nice people, and even a few neighborhood dogs, but never did come across Liberty. Fish had no idea where she managed to hide, out of sight, for so long. He wished he could invent something that would find a missing dog. Maybe he'd go through those old *Popular Mechanics* magazines tonight, after supper. Might be an idea in one of those.

"I gotta get home," Olympia said when the Catholic church bells chimed five. "I'm sorry we got skunked. But, like Grandmamma says, if at first you don't succeed, try, try again."

Fish nodded. That was like what the president said in that fireside chat. But they'd tried so many times. Maybe he had to face facts. He wasn't going to find Liberty. It had been silly to think he would. Just like it was silly to think he could fix his leg. "You tell Miss Zona I'll bring the trap over tomorrow night. She can keep it as long as she needs. I don't think I'm ever going to catch that dog." He hadn't felt this low since that first night in the polio ward.

Olympia stopped dead-still on the banquette. "Don't say that. Remember what that Mr. Churchill said? 'Never ever ever give up.'" She crossed her arms. "That dog will come to you again. I just know it. Grandmamma feels it in her bones, too."

Fish wished he had Olympia's confidence. "See you tomorrow." He went inside the house and did his stretching exercises, just in case Olympia was right about that never-giving-up thing. He used Mo's sewing tape measure to check for progress, but his right leg was still an inch shorter than his left. It hadn't lengthened one iota and the knee was as frozen as ever. Nothing was going to turn out right. Not the leg or the dog.

Someone knocked on the front door. *Shave and a haircut.* He peeked over Pop's Blue Star Flag. Olympia stood on the front porch.

"I brought you a plate," she said through the glass. "Fried chicken and mashed taters."

He yanked open the door.

Olympia handed him the covered dish, lowering her voice. "I told Grandmamma about that liver curry. She said no human being should have to eat such. Especially as leftovers!"

"Tell Miss Zona my stomach and I are grateful." Fish inhaled the delicious smells. "Very grateful!"

Olympia skipped down the stairs. "You can set the plate on our porch when you're done. To hide the evidence." She laughed.

Fish savored each bite of crispy chicken and buttery potatoes as he pored over several of those old *Popular Mechanics* he'd found in the shed. They gave him lots of good ideas — how to build his own radio and chick brooder and crossbow to "shoot arrows or launch airplanes." Mo would have conniptions about the last two things. But nothing that gave him any ideas about inventing a gizmo to find a lost dog. He did have all the supplies to make the radio, so after getting rid of his chicken dinner evidence, he gathered them together and started to work. He was winding wire around a paper clip when the front door lock rattled.

"Are you still up?" Mo took off her hat, yawning. "It's past your bedtime."

"Can I finish this part?" He showed her what he was doing.

"You and your inventions." Mo opened the icebox. "Looks like you ate a good supper," she said.

Fish had taken precautions, scooping out more of the leftovers into the trap to make it seem like he'd eaten them. Not even the starvingest child in China would eat liver curry.

"Still hungry?" She held out the plate.

"Oh, no, thanks." Fish patted his stomach. "Full up."

Mo put it back and pulled out a milk bottle, pouring herself a glass as she kicked off her pumps. "What a day!" She plopped onto a kitchen chair. "You were the talk of the meeting."

Fish stopped winding. "What?"

She took a sip, swallowing and nodding her head at the same time. "I've been getting to know one of the engineers, Mr. Haddock. A real nice guy who's giving me tips on becoming an engineer." Mo had taken the job at Higgins hoping she could put her mechanical background to work — she'd grown up working with Pop in Uncle Dutch's garage — but the rule was that women could work in the plant, not in engineering. That was just one of the work rules Fish didn't understand. Higgins also kept separate assembly lines for the white and the black workers, even though everybody seemed to get along. Mo said that kind of stuff was sure to change after the war. "It has to," she said. "We're fighting for freedom, aren't we?" At any rate, she'd taken the secretarial job hoping it would give her an in for her engineering dream. Like most of Mo's plans, it seemed to be working.

Mo rolled her neck side to side, stretching out kinks. "I told him how proud I was of you and that I thought you were going to be the next Thomas Edison."

"Oh, yeah." Fish blew a raspberry.

"I took that cigar box contraption of yours to show him." Mo rubbed her temples. "Gosh, what a long day."

Fish had wondered where he'd left that. Olympia was fussing about getting her hair ribbons back. "What did he say?"

Mo stopped rubbing, looking Fish square in the face. "You might be more interested in what someone else had to say."

"Cut the mystery. Please."

"You know how I told you there was this big wrinkle at work? I can't tell you everything — top secret — but it had to do with the ramps on the boats that will carry the tanks. Tank lighters, they're called. Getting them to lower in a less complicated way. Mr. Higgins shut all the engineers in the office, saying they couldn't leave until they figured it out. Someone tried to go get a sandwich at lunchtime and Mr. Higgins ordered him back inside and sent me out for food. While I was gone, one of the guys noticed your cigar box on my desk. He started playing around with it and then someone else said, 'Hey, that gives me an idea.'" Mo beamed. "Your model got those engineers thinking in a different way. And they solved the problem! Mr. Higgins was so happy, he passed cigars all around. Even to me!"

"Are you pulling my leg?" Fish's contraption helped the most important shipyard in America?

Mo crossed her heart. "It's the honest truth." She patted the table between them. "And now, Mr. Brilliant, it's way past time for you to hit the hay."

Fish nearly brushed his teeth with Mo's face cream, he was so astonished at her story. He crawled under the sheets, staring at the ceiling, while that delicious thought played over and over: His model had inspired real engineers! As he drifted off to sleep, he realized the best part. He'd done something that would make Pop proud.

He couldn't wait to write to tell him.

CHAPTER SEVEN

Roll Call

They were rousted out for the daily roll call. Erich found his spot in the long line with many hundred other prisoners. It would be ages before the last name was ticked off. The sun's heat battered the tops of heads like a sledge-hammer. After the first hour, Erich could not conjure up enough saliva to lick his blistered lips. The man next to him swayed, nearly knock-ing Erich off his feet. Erich pushed him upright and held him there till the man was able to stand on his own again. The man nodded thanks; speaking required too much effort.

Erich would not fall. He loosened his knees, relaxing his body as best he could. He thought back to his father teaching him to ski. "It's all in the knees, son," Vater had told him. If he closed his eyes, Erich could almost imagine shushing over the snow, flying free. When Friedrich had been born, Erich looked forward to teaching his brother to ski. But Friedrich's leg made that impossible.

Erich did his best to keep his family at the front of his thoughts; it helped to block out the heat, the flies, the angry Frog guard calling off the German names as slowly as possible. He hoped Mutti did not worry too much about him. He hoped his father was still playing the piano of an evening. And Friedrich — was he keeping up with his chess? One of the first things Erich would do when he returned home was set up the board. Perhaps this time, his little brother would beat him. Fair and square.

Finally, the last name was called. "Roll call, dismissed!" shouted the guard. Erich staggered after his fellows to the mess tent. He ate. Not for himself. But to survive for his family. For Friedrich.

CHAPTER EIGHT

No Picnic at the Beach

Mo clattered around in the kitchen, waking Fish from a really good dream. He and Liberty were playing fetch and no matter how far he threw the ball, she caught it and brought it back. "Good girl," he mumbled as he rolled over.

The door to his room popped open, letting in breakfast smells. Bacon. Pancakes. Maple syrup.

"Up and at 'em, sleepyhead." Mo waved a spatula at him. "We need to leave in an hour to meet Roy."

Fish pulled the bedspread over his head. He'd forgotten about the day at the beach. "I might not feel very good," he fibbed. He definitely wouldn't feel very good if he went another day without catching Liberty. Except for the night in Miss Zona's garden, the trap had been baited every day with something tasty. Yesterday, he and Olympia had put out chipped beef.

"You'll feel better after some food." Mo poked him with the spatula. "Let's go." She closed the door behind her as she stepped back into the kitchen.

Fish threw off the covers and climbed out of bed to do his stretching exercises. Push, count, hold. Push, count, hold. Sweat trickled down his back as he worked to get his knee to bend. The pain would be worth it, if he could change that leg. He paused, studying the stiffened knee. Was it a little bit more flexible? Maybe a tiny bit.

"You do look flushed," Mo said as he sat at the table.

Fish realized he probably overdid it with the stretching. "Uh, I forgot to open my window last night. It got really hot in my room."

She reached over and felt his forehead anyway. "No fever, but warm." She poured him a glass of milk. "This will cool you off. The window's a good idea. It's supposed to hit ninety today."

After breakfast, he and Mo headed to the streetcar stop. They waved to Miss Zona and Olympia on their front porch, all dolled up for church, waiting for Mr. Simpson. Fish had never met Mr. Simpson, only seen him coming down the street in his Plymouth coupe, barely visible behind the dashboard. The way he looked reminded Fish of the time he tried to be helpful and do some laundry for Mo. He'd washed one of her wool sweaters in hot water and it came out baby doll–sized. Mr. Simpson looked like he'd been shrunk in the wash, too, wrinkly and small. Even though he was about ninety, every Sunday morning, at exactly 10:15, he picked up their neighbors for church, insisting on parking his car and escorting Miss Zona down the front steps. They looked like Mutt and Jeff from the funny papers. It was a wonder Mr. Simpson didn't fall right over.

Fish step-clomped alongside Mo to the corner. Her lips and nails were cherry red and she smelled of Shalimar, too dressed up for the beach. But he said, "You look nice."

The first streetcar that passed said COLORED ONLY, but another one came along in a few minutes. They paid their seven cents fare, getting transfers from the conductorette. At the end of the streetcar line, they transferred to a bus and soon were mingling with the crowds at Pontchartrain Beach.

The air felt like a damp washcloth on Fish's face. He looked up. Would it be another one of those days where the skies opened up in the afternoon?

"I want to try on a gas mask," Mo said. Fish followed her to a line of people waiting to pay a nickel for that pleasure. Fish watched as the lady in front of him gave it a go. He wondered if Pop ever had to wear one. He hoped not. In his last letter to Mo, Pop said that he was safer as a combat engineer than he'd been as a mechanic.

Some news photographer from the *Times-Picayune* snapped a photo of Mo when it was her turn to try on the gas mask. The reporter tagging along asked for her name and how to spell it. "How's about a phone number, too, Toots?" The reporter winked.

Mo slipped off the mask, fluffing her hair before handing it to Fish. "Move along," she told the reporter. "My boyfriend will be here any minute."

The reporter shrugged. "Can't blame a guy for trying."

Mo glared at him. "Just watch me."

The photographer nudged the reporter. "Let's get a shot over there." They wandered off.

"Fresh." Mo shook her head. "Don't be like that when you grow up, Fish. Okay?"

Fish had no problem agreeing. That girl-boy stuff gave him the willies. He slipped the mask over his head. It was heavier than he thought it would be. And stuffier. How did people breathe with one of those on? He couldn't wait to take it off and hand it back to the lady Red Cross volunteer, who said,

"The kids in Hawaii have to carry these everywhere. Can you imagine?"

Fish shook his head. He could not imagine. Though he wouldn't mind if Wally had to wear one. That would make their classroom a lot quieter. "Hey, look over there." He pointed to a booth that said SEND YOUR SOLDIER A VOICE-O-GRAPH, SPONSORED BY GEM BLADES AND RAZORS.

"You want to do that for Pop?" Mo asked.

Fish watched as a lady went inside the booth. Soon he could hear her singing "They Can't Take That Away from Me." Her voice cracked as she repeated the last line of the song and she was wiping her eyes as she stepped out of the booth. Another lady grabbed her in a hug and they stood, sniffling, while waiting for her record to be pressed.

"That guy can go first." Fish pointed to a man in a seersucker suit. Watching that lady got Fish all choked up. If he sent a message to Pop, he wanted it to be loud and clear. Strong and straight. Just like his leg was going to be.

Whatever the seersucker suit man recorded, Fish couldn't hear it. So that gave him time to think of what to say to Pop. The sign said the recordings took two minutes. "Do you want to do it with me?" he asked Mo. What if he couldn't think of two minutes of stuff to talk about?

"The booth looks too small for two people." Mo handed him the thirty-five cents. "You make a record for Pop. I want to make one for Roy to take with him when he ships out." Assuming Captain McDerby passed him, Roy would be on his way to San Diego in a few weeks.

The man in the seersucker suit stepped out. "Next!" He smiled at Fish.

The volunteer working the booth shut the door after Fish stepped inside. An instruction sheet was pasted on the wall in front of him, and a money slot sat below a small shelf about waist high. A clipboard was chained to the shelf with a note: IT HELPS TO JOT DOWN YOUR THOUGHTS FIRST! Fish ignored that. Talking was going to be challenging enough. He skimmed the set of instructions pasted on the wall: DROP COINS IN SLOT. WATCH FOR SIGNAL LIGHTS BELOW, THEN TALK INTO MICROPHONE. He stood six inches from the microphone, as the sign instructed. When he slid his dime and quarter into the slot, something clicked and began to whir. The START READING bar lit up. Panicked, Fish backed away from the microphone, bumping into the booth door.

"You okay in there?" Mo called.

"Yeah." Fish shook himself, then scanned the list of suggestions: SING YOUR FAVORITE SONG. Fish couldn't carry a tune in a bucket. SEND A GREETING TO YOUR RELATION. Okay. "Hey, hello, Pop," Fish started. He cleared his throat, reading down the suggestion list. TALK ABOUT WHERE YOU ARE, WHO YOU ARE WITH, AND WHAT YOU ARE DOING. "Hi, it's Fish. Me and Mo are at the beach today. We're going to see Roy later and get a ride in an LCVP. You know, landing craft, vehicle, personnel." Swallow. "Are you doing okay, Pop? We are." Pause. "Guess what? Mo took one of my gadgets to work and it gave the engineers an idea for improving a tank lighter. To make it easier to raise and lower the exit ramp. It was just something I made out of a cigar box and some junk. What do you think about that?"

Fish tried to imagine Pop's face when he listened to this news. Mo said Pop had a poker face. It was hard to know what he was thinking by watching his expressions. But maybe his eyes would light up like they did when Ted Williams hit a homer, or when Pop laid down a pinochle during a game of cards. Maybe the news would help Pop forget about Fish's leg. For a little while, at least.

Another bar lit up; thirty seconds left. "Anyway, Pop. We can't wait till you come home." Fish paused again. "Forward, Pop! Keep building those bridges. We miss you. Bye for now."

The STOP RECORDING light blipped on. He'd done it! Fish swiped at his forehead as he stepped out of the booth.

"Warm in there?" Mo asked.

"Yeah." Warm, but also it was hard work. How did those radio announcers blab away all the time like they did? Fish was glad inventors didn't have to do a lot of talking.

It took only a few minutes for his record to be pressed. The six-inch vinyl disc was still warm when the volunteer handed it to him. He slipped the record into the cardboard envelope, holding the whole thing very carefully. It had a long way to travel to get to Pop.

The booth door swung open. Mo stepped out, a wistful expression on her face.

"You okay?" Fish asked.

She shrugged. "It just brought it all home. Roy's really leaving."

Fish awkwardly patted his sister's arm, hoping she wasn't going to start blubbering like that other lady. He couldn't handle tears. Especially not Mo's.

Mo took her record from the man at the booth and slid it into an envelope and then into her pocketbook. "Want me to hold on to yours, too?"

Fish handed it over. "Let's mail it tomorrow."

"I can do that from the office." Mo snapped her pocketbook shut. "Time to find Roy." They shuffled across patches of sand and grass to the lake's edge. Three LCVPs were lined up on the beach. And all the sailors in the ships looked identical. Fish couldn't pick Roy out.

"He's in number 94." Mo shielded her eyes from the sun to study the numbers painted on the sides of the boats.

"There it is!" Fish led the way to the farthest landing craft, Mo following right behind.

Roy saw them coming and waved his arm like he was the King of Mardi Gras on a float. "Come aboard," he called out.

The ramp at the bow of the boat had been lowered. Fish and Mo scrambled up, along with some other people. Fish knew that the soldiers didn't come aboard this way; they clambered up the thick netting of ropes fastened on the side. A few more people meandered up the ramp and then a sailor on the beach held up his hand, making the rest of the folks wait for the next ride. Roy raised the ramp and it groaned to a close, clanking so hard that Fish could feel the vibration in his chest. As the boat backed off the beach, the engineer gave a little spiel, shouting over the engine, wind, and water. They roared out onto the lake. Mo and the other ladies clamped their hats to their heads with one hand and hung on with the other.

"This landing craft was built right here in New Orleans, by a little company called Higgins Industries." The engineer laughed at his own bad joke. A few of the passengers chuckled, knowing full well that Higgins Industries was anything but small, with two huge plants in New Orleans alone. "It's built of a mix of oak, pine, and mahogany, protected by steel armor on the hull. This workhorse can carry thirty-six troops, or three tons of vehicles. She's probably clipping along now at about ten knots, right, Skipper?" He looked over at Roy, who nodded. "But she can top out at twelve knots unloaded, nine knots fully loaded. And it only takes four geniuses to run her: the coxswain there" — he pointed at Roy, then at himself — "an engineer like me, and two crew. Who wants to guess what they do?"

Mo nudged Fish. He could give this talk in his sleep, Mo had told him so much about all the different boats being built at Higgins. "Man the machine guns," Fish called out.

"That's right." The engineer nodded. "Those babies right there." Some kid tried to climb up to touch the machine guns, but the engineer stopped him. "Those aren't toys, tiger." He shooed the kid back to his parents.

Roy and the coxswains of the other two LCVPs — now on the water, too — slowed to form a circle, puttering behind one another. "This is one of our evasive maneuvers," Roy explained, shouting over the engine noise. "Kind of like the settlers circling their wagons in the Old West."

As tall as he was, even standing on his toes, Fish couldn't see over the sides of the landing craft. But he could feel the wind and smell the brackish lake water. That's what it would be like for the men riding in this boat on their way to a beach landing somewhere. They would be blind to where they were going. What they were headed into. Only the coxswain — and the gunners — would be able to see what the troops were facing. It was warm in the boat, with the sun reflecting off the water, but that thought made Fish shiver as he studied Roy, standing straight and tall in his crisp uniform.

A funny feeling came over Fish. Soon, Roy wouldn't be doing practice runs or tourist trips on the lake here. He'd be on a ship, maybe heading to the Pacific. Steaming to danger.

Roy caught Fish looking at him and gave a thumbs-up. Fish returned the gesture. Then Roy circled his finger in the air, asking, "Ready to head in?"

Fish shook his head. Out here, the war was at bay. He liked that feeling.

Roy grinned and the engine roared; he pulled out of the circle and cut through the water like a great shark. Fish lost his balance and grabbed on to one of the exposed ribs. The energy of the boat's thrust pushed him back, but he found a way to lean on his good leg. Wind whipped around his face, making his eyes water, ruffling his hair. He felt like Errol Flynn in one of those pirate movies. He tilted his head back, hollering at a pair of pelicans flying overhead. "Avast, me hearties!" Mo laughed. Too soon, Roy wheeled the boat around. Toward shore.

"Watch him nail this landing," the engineer shouted in Fish's ear. "You can tip these things like nobody's business if you breech 'em even one tiny bit." He grinned big. "Roy always hits it straight and high." He whooped. "Ride her in, cowboy!"

The shore barreled at them. Fish steeled himself for a crash. He might have even closed his eyes. With a whoosh and a whump, Roy placed the bow of the craft square on the beach. Everyone cheered. Especially Fish. Roy tipped his hat, then lowered the ramp.

Fish's legs wobbled as he made his way off the landing craft.

Mo's eyes sparkled. "Wasn't that great?"

Fish nodded. It had been. Except for thinking about Roy driving an LCVP in the war, landing it somewhere like Tarawa or Guadalcanal, where there had been big battles. Big casualties. Fish decided he wasn't going to complain about setting three plates at the table anymore.

"I'm famished!" Mo resettled her hat and smoothed out her flyaway hair. "Roy's got some more runs to do before he can take us home. How about lunch?"

They ate two hot dogs each and shared a Dr. Nut soda, then strolled to the far end of the beach, where they found a snowball stand to cool off. Mo tried mint, but Fish stuck with grape. They strolled back toward the landing crafts and were finishing their treats when Roy found them. He stopped to buy a hot dog for himself, which he ate on the way to the car.

"A penny for your thoughts?" Roy studied Fish in the rearview mirror as they cruised down Elysian Fields.

"That was great." Fish leaned back against the seat. "Really great."

Roy glanced over his shoulder, face serious. "I was glad to do it, Fish."

Mo fiddled with the car radio. An Andrews Sisters song came on. "I can't help singing along," she said. "Even though I'm tone-deaf."

"You don't have to tell us!" Roy teased, catching Fish's eye in the rearview mirror again with a wink.

Mo pretended to pout.

Fish smiled. Maybe boy-girl stuff wasn't so bad after all. For Mo and Roy.

A slight figure sat, hunched over, on their front porch when they pulled up.

"Hey, Olympia." Mo and Roy headed inside.

"I've got news." Olympia tugged him around to the backyard. "Look."

The pie tin was empty.

"She was here and I missed her!" Fish slapped at the cage in frustration. Of all the days for Liberty to eat the food in the trap. Then he stopped for a second. "Why didn't the door close?" He'd been so sure his plan would work.

Olympia tugged on the braid closest to her face. "That's the news."

Fish picked up the pie tin. He'd wash it out and refill it right after supper. "What news?"

"I was only trying to help." Olympia started tugging on a second braid. "Honest."

He banged the pie tin against his thigh. "Spit it out, for crying out loud."

"The good news is that your trap worked fine." She tried out a smile. "Liberty took the bait like we planned and the door snapped shut."

Fish leaned against the live oak. "Then why isn't she in there?"

Olympia hung her head and sighed deeply. "I let her out."

"Let her —"

"It wasn't like that." Olympia perched on a pile of lumber, like a bird poised for flight. "She seemed so scared. I wanted to pet her. Calm her down. Let her know we wouldn't hurt her."

Fish picked a bent nail out of the dirt. "And when you opened the door, she got out." He flipped the nail toward the trash can.

"I was only trying to help." Olympia wouldn't even meet Fish's gaze.

Fish shifted his attention to the empty cage. So close. He turned toward the back steps. "Do me a favor, will you?"

"Anything." Olympia looked up. "I am so sorry."

"Don't help me." Fish clumped up the first step. "I mean it. I don't want your help. Anymore."

When he reached the top, he jerked open the screen door, letting it slam shut behind him. He heard Miss Zona call Olympia home.

Good riddance.

CHAPTER NINE

Putting Pen to Paper

Fish hated math bees. Especially when it was boys against girls. The girls had solved three problems while Wally was at the board. It took all of Fish's willpower not to shout out the answer. Couldn't Wally see it?

Lurelle hurried up to the blackboard after Audrey tagged her. Fish dropped his head to his desk. The boys were going to lose. Again.

"Finished!" Lurelle put the chalk in the tray and brushed her hands. "The answer is ninety-seven."

"Nicely done, ladies." Mrs. Francis made a tally mark in the far corner of the blackboard. "It looks like the boys are lagging a bit. The score this year is girls 20, boys 16." She clucked her tongue. "Some of you young men need to spend more time on math facts and less on comic books."

Wally kicked the back of Fish's chair. "I thought you were such an egghead."

"I can't win all by myself." Fish scooted his chair forward, out of reach of Wally's foot.

"Do I hear talking?" Mrs. Francis scoured the room. No one uttered a peep. "Good." She turned her back to the class and began writing on the board. "One of my favorite assignments each year is coming right up." She wrote *Monday May 29, 1944: Memorial Day* on the board. "You will write an original essay. The topic is" — she chalked it out in her perfect Palmer Method penmanship — "My Hero." She faced the class, beaming. "I know you will write some wonderful and heartfelt essays. And here is the best part!"

Fish thought his teacher might faint dead away with pleasure.

"Principal Sellars will select three to read aloud over the school's public address system, in celebration of the holiday."

Fish doubted that any of his classmates, except

maybe Lurelle, were as overjoyed as Mrs. Francis at this announcement. Sure enough, Lurelle's hand shot straight up.

"One more thing before I get to your questions." Mrs. Francis adjusted her bifocals on her nose. "I will need all the essays a week from Friday."

"I'm going to write about my big brother who's in the Navy," Wally called out. "He's knocking the heil out of Hitler!" Several of the boys laughed.

"Raise your hand before speaking, please, Wallace."

Wally raised his hand. Mrs. Francis called on him. He repeated what he had just said, except for the heil part.

Ernie flapped his arm around. "Can I write about my cousin? He's in the Coast Guard."

Mrs. Francis nodded. "Of course."

Lurelle's hand shot up again. "Mrs. Francis, can a hero be a woman?"

"Oh, my, yes." Mrs. Francis's eyes got even bigger behind her bifocal lenses. "I know I am going to be so pleased with these essays."

She patted her palm on her desk top. "I hope to see equal enthusiasm about our vocabulary assignment." Mrs. Francis motioned to pull out spelling books.

Fish dutifully copied down the week's list. While Mrs. Francis related "fascinating facts" about the origins of each word, he doodled in the margin of his paper. At first it was just a scribble, but the blip in the center looked like a nose. A dog's nose. He added two ears, folded down in little triangles, soft as Mo's cashmere sweater, and big eyes. Big brown eyes.

Liberty.

It'd been weeks since Fish had seen her. He hadn't spoken to Olympia in all that time. She kept popping her head through the fence, but he went inside the minute she did. He wouldn't even answer the door when she brought over a plate of Miss Zona's fudge to add to their care packages to Pop and Roy. She couldn't have left well enough alone when Liberty was in the trap. She had to go and try and pet her.

Fish pulled a pink eraser out of his desk and furiously rubbed out his drawing. Good-bye, Liberty. He hoped someone was taking care of her. Giving her plenty to eat. Keeping her safe.

The bell chimed for the end of the day. Mrs. Francis held up her hands, holding up their exit. "Before you go, students, there is one more thing. I want to know your essay topic before you begin writing. You may tell me in the morning."

The thought of writing an essay hung over Fish like a dark cloud all the way home. Words were so slippery. He had a hard time getting them from his head to the page. And if he got another D in language arts, Mo would — well, he didn't know what she might do. But it wouldn't be good. That much he did know. His step-clomps were slower than ever as he walked and worried.

The mailbox held a bit of blue sky. A postcard

from Roy. Nothing from Pop, but they'd gotten a letter a few days back. It was like most all the other letters: *"I'll send more money. Take care. I'm fine. Pop."* Roy, on the other hand, could write. Fish enjoyed the postcards most because they were right there for him to read, too. This latest card was postmarked Tombstone: *"You wouldn't think so, but the desert is beautiful. I feel no bigger than a crawfish when I think about how big this country of ours is. I say we all explore it together when this war is over! Take good care, you two. Love, Roy."* Fish had dug out an old atlas and was tracing Roy's route, inking a little dot for each place he mentioned. Now Fish added one for Tombstone. He'd already put one at San Diego, where Roy would finish his training. Fish ran his finger between the starting dot and ending dot. A lot of miles. He kept the map in his room; seeing it might only make Mo feel worse.

She had been a low-volume version of herself since Roy shipped out. She and Roy had celebrated his graduation from the Higgins training — Captain

McDerby passed him, after all, in spite of all the times he got on Roy — at the Roosevelt Hotel on a Friday night, and by Monday, Roy was on a train to San Diego. After that, Mo still did everything she always did, but with less spark and sparkle. Suppers were lonely with only two plates on the table.

Fish noticed the Blue Star Flag Mo bought as soon as Roy shipped out. It was lying on the counter; she planned to hang it that weekend. He'd surprise her. Hang it right now, next to Pop's, so she could see it tonight first thing when she got home. That might perk her up.

The hammer and nails were in the shed, on a shelf on the far wall, over the bicycle, which he'd left uncovered. He couldn't avoid noticing that it was in good condition. Flat tires were fixable. He remembered Nurse Meg and how there was this one therapy exercise where she'd forced his right leg to move around and around. Kind of like pedaling a bike. Maybe he *could* ride again. Maybe that would help his leg more than his latest exercise contraption, which hadn't made a noticeable difference at all. Fish wheeled the bike out into the yard so he could work on it after he got the flag up. He tacked the flag to the rail in the middle of the front door window, next to Pop's, making sure it was hanging straight. Then he returned to the backyard.

Buried under a dozen old coffee cans in the shed, he found a pump and added air to the bike's tires. Then he leaned the bike against the live oak tree, looking it over. At five, he'd hopped right on his birthday bike. Didn't think twice about falling, crashing. But both legs had worked fine then.

With the bike still supported by the tree, Fish mounted. Got a feel for the seat. They said a person never forgot how to ride a bicycle. He rocked back and forth, reminding himself how it felt to be balanced over two wheels. When he felt comfortable, he straightened his left arm, pushing himself away from the tree. Without any forward momentum, the bike wobbled wildly. After experimenting, he found that if he rotated his right hip, he could hook his heel at the very edge of the pedal. His left leg would have to do all the work, but with the right foot tucked in like this, he felt more stable. Ready to give it a go. When he pushed again on the pedal with his left leg, his right foot flew off the other side. But he rolled forward. He pushed again with his left leg and covered a little more ground.

He practiced going around the yard a couple times, but it was so small, the sharp turns kicked him off. Without letting himself think about it too much, he pointed the bike toward the banquette in front of the house. And he kept going. Down Fig Street, crossing at Eagle, and up Fig again.

"You look familiar!" Miss Rose called out as he passed Cali's Market for the third time. She laughed and waved and returned to arranging bananas. Fish waved, too, wobbled, then clamped both hands back on the handlebars. He kept riding up and down the street. Once he got a rhythm going, he began to relax. To breathe. Maybe if he could handle riding a bike, he could handle the essay for Mrs. Francis. He even began to think about a topic. Brainstorming like those engineers at Higgins Industries with his cigar box. His invention had helped them think of something new. Even Mr. Higgins had been impressed.

Mr. Andrew Jackson Higgins. If there was a bigger hero in New Orleans, Fish couldn't think who it would be. The more he thought about it, the more he thought he had come up with an A+ idea.

He'd need Mo's help getting an appointment with Mr. Higgins. She'd say yes, of course. It was for school, after all. And she always made the appointments for her boss, so that part should be a cinch.

Fish rolled up to their front walk, hop-hop-hopping along till the bike slowed. Stopped. He was winded but happy. Riding was sure to make a difference for his leg. He whistled as he wheeled the bike into the backyard.

Liberty was curled up under the live oak.

With blood all over her side.

CHAPTER TEN

Hitching a Ride

For the third day in a row, Erich listened to the Americans shout out names of other men from the Afrika Korps and watched as those men jumped into trucks and rode off across the desert. Rumor had it they were going to camps in the States, where there was plenty of good food. And not one French guard.

From his vantage point near the fence, as close to the trucks as he could get, Erich took note. German prisoners were called, one after another. They got waved onto trucks. But never once did Erich see anyone request or present identification.

He did not think he had the courage to act on his own. Oskar, sick of the Frogs and their many small but pointed ways of making the prisoners' lives as miserable as possible, quickly jumped at Erich's idea. "We all look alike in these rags anyway," Oskar said. "What's the worst they could do if they catch you?" He snorted. "Send you to a prison camp?"

It was decided. They would make their move the next day. In the morning, a stocky American sergeant stood at the gate in the wire fence. He called out several dozen names: "Acker, Baumgartner, Fertig, Klein, Metzler, Richter, Volk." The Professor's name was called and he made his way stiffly toward the gate, suffering as he did from a shrapnel wound that had not healed properly. Erich signaled Oskar and they hastened to his side, each offering an arm to the older man. Each nodding at the sergeant as they passed through the gate, away from the French, away from the desert, away from Algiers.

The men already seated on the hard plank seats in the truck merely moved over to make room for three more.

Nothing was said. No questions were asked.

Erich allowed himself a smile. The first in a long time.

Whatever awaited him in the United States, he was ready for it.

CHAPTER ELEVEN

Forward Fish

Fish approached slowly. Liberty lifted her head, brown eyes dull with pain.

"It's okay, girl. I'm going to help you." The blood was dried. Crusted. Maybe it wasn't as bad as it looked. He kept talking to her, kept easing closer. At the base of the tree, he stiffly lowered himself to the ground. She shied away a bit at his clumsy movements, so he rested his hand on her head. "Good girl. Good girl."

Liberty turned to lick his hand.

Without touching her side, Fish inspected the wound, which was jagged but not deep. Maybe she got caught on some barbed wire. He stroked her head again. She snuffled, tucking her muzzle between her front paws. He didn't want to leave her. But he needed to get her cleaned up. Maybe put something on the gash.

The sound of the fence board sliding caught the back side of his thoughts. Then, Olympia was next to him, setting down a basin of soapy water. She pulled some rags from her skirt pocket.

He took one of the rags, dipped it in the basin, and gently washed Liberty's side. She didn't make a sound, keeping her eyes fixed on him. Trusting him to help her. Trusting him completely.

"Looks like your dog got herself in a fight," Olympia said.

"Is that what happened, girl? A fight?" It figured there would be dog bullies in the world, just like there were people bullies. "It's okay now. You're okay." Fish rinsed the rag, wringing it out. The water in the basin turned pink. "Do you think we should put something on it? Some ointment?"

"Want me to ask Grandmamma? She's doctored plenty of people."

Fish checked Liberty over while Olympia was gone. Aside from being dirty and infested with fleas, it didn't seem like she was hurt anywhere else. He found one little chunk out of her right ear, but that looked like an old injury. "You've had a rough life, haven't you, girl?" He scratched between her eyes. She huffed, lay her head down, and relaxed.

Olympia wiggled back through the gap in the fence. In one hand, she carried a brown bottle. Mercurochrome. In the other, a jar of some kind of salve. "Grandmamma says after we get it washed off, clean it with this" — she waggled the bottle — "and then slather on some of this." She held up the jar. "It's her own special salve. Stinks but it works."

Fish finished cleaning up the blood. "Maybe I should hold on to her and you put on the Mercurochrome." He didn't want to be the one to do anything that might hurt. And he knew from all the skinned knees he got, learning to walk again, how much Mercurochrome could sting.

Olympia dabbed at Liberty's side with the brown

stuff. The dog wiggled a bit, then shifted around, laying her head in Fish's lap. He thought his heart might crumble. He was never going to let anything bad happen to Liberty again. Ever. He rested his hand on her soft head.

"I think I got it good." Olympia screwed the top back on the bottle. "Do you want to do this?" She held out the jar of salve.

Fish wanted to, but Liberty seemed so comfortable with her head in his lap. "Naw. I don't want to move."

"This is good practice for me." Olympia patted a layer of goo on Liberty's side. "I want to be a nurse. Like my auntie, in the Army Nurse Corps." She wiped her hands off on one of the clean rags. "She's in England right now. Doing her bit." Pride washed over Olympia's words.

"I didn't know that." Fish scratched under Liberty's chin. The dog was now sound asleep. She must've been completely worn out. "About your aunt or about you wanting to be a nurse."

Olympia shrugged. "Probably lots you don't know about me."

She was right about that. "Hey, thanks. For doing all this."

"That's what neighbors are for." She began picking up the first-aid supplies. "Grandmamma says we're just taking up space unless we're doing unto others." She started back for the gap in the fence. "Plus, I owe you."

"I'm going to need some dog supplies," Fish blurted out. "A collar. A leash. Want to go to Mr. Campbell's with me later?"

Olympia answered with a smile. "Let's stop at Cali's Market and ask for some bones, too." As she slipped through the fence, he heard her holler. "I'll be back quick as I can!"

Liberty twitched in her sleep. Maybe she was dreaming about chasing rabbits. He was going to have to read up about dogs. He wanted to be the best master ever. Make Liberty forget she'd ever been lost and alone.

Olympia came back with some scraps from Miss Zona. Liberty woke up and wolfed them down. "You're just plain starving, aren't you, baby?" Olympia cooed at Liberty, stroking her ears.

The back door creaked open. "And what is going on here?" Mo asked.

"She's hurt," Fish said.

"Who does she belong to?" Mo unpinned her hat.

Fish glanced over at Olympia. She nodded encouragement. He swallowed. "Me, I hope."

Mo's mouth opened, then closed. "I cannot process this information without a Coca-Cola." She held up a finger before disappearing into the house.

"You didn't tell her about the dog?" Olympia whispered.

"What would I have said?" Dogs were definitely on the Do Not Tell Mo list. "I didn't know I'd catch Liberty. Not for sure."

Olympia merely shook her head.

Mo returned, dressed in capris and a sleeveless

blouse, holding an icy bottle in her hand. She sat down on the porch, shuffling her bare feet against the steps. "I suppose I'm going to have to loan you money for dog supplies." She took a sip of her Coke.

"I'll do extra chores," Fish offered. "She's really sweet. Want to come pet her?"

"Not till she's had a bath. I can see the fleas jumping from here."

"She's not so bad." Fish crossed his fingers behind his back.

Mo stretched out her legs. "Rule number one." She waggled the bottle for emphasis. "No dogs in the house."

Olympia dragged over an old washtub from her grandmother's basement. Using bits of leftover frankfurter, Fish lured Liberty into the tub. She got in but would not sit down. They scooped water up in old coffee cans and poured it over her. Fish hoped Mo would stay on the steps. If she came any closer, she'd see the army of fleas floating in the dirty water.

Fish hated to do it, but he had to tie Liberty up so he could go get some basic canine supplies. Seemed like the bath had worn her out; she curled up and was snoring little doggy snores in no time. Mo hardly grumbled at all as she handed over a couple of dollars, and Fish and Olympia high-tailed it to the store.

Mr. Campbell was surprised when Fish put the collar and the leash on the counter. "You got a dog now?" he asked.

Before Fish could even answer, Olympia jumped in. "She's smart as a whip, too. Name's Liberty."

"Good name." Mr. Campbell nodded his approval. "Seems like you'd best get out to my scrap pile and see if I've got enough bits to build your Liberty a doghouse."

Fish hadn't even thought about that. He thanked Mr. Campbell, who handed over an issue of *Popular Mechanics* along with the leash and collar. "You'll find a dandy set of plans in here."

After they got back from Mr. Campbell's, Miss Zona called for Olympia to come on in. She didn't run home till she gave Liberty a big hug and kiss. "You sleep tight, girl. I'll bring you some bacon in the morning!"

Fish cleared out a spot in the shed for Liberty to sleep until he got the doghouse built. He provisioned it with food and water and an old blanket. She got a little antsy when he started to close the shed door. "I'll be back first thing," he promised. "This is to keep you safe tonight." He tossed in a Milk-Bone and wrestled the door shut. It didn't sit right on its hinges. It about broke his heart to hear her scratching to get out. He didn't blame her for hating to be closed up in there. He'd have to do something about that right away.

He pored over the doghouse plans at the kitchen table. It was going to take him some time to build this. Liberty wouldn't like being in the shed that long. He'd best come up with a plan B. Mo looked up from the letter she was writing to Roy. "That dog better not interfere with your schoolwork," she warned.

Schoolwork! He'd almost forgotten about the essay. He needed to tell Mrs. Francis his topic in the morning. "About that," he said. "I have an idea for a big assignment, but I need your help." He asked Mo about interviewing Mr. Higgins.

"Well, he's pretty busy," she said. "But I'll see what I can do. Especially since we don't want any more notes home from your teacher." Mo arched her eyebrows at him before pulling a piece of paper from the stack next to her. "Speaking of writing, I bet Pop would like to hear about the newest member of the family."

Fish usually struggled with what to say to his father. He couldn't write about sports or anything like that. But he quickly had a page full of words, telling about Liberty and taking care of her and plans for the doghouse. He left out the part about riding the bike. He never liked to say anything that reminded Pop about his leg.

He finished the letter, and signed it with the motto of his dad's battalion: *"Forward, Fish."*

CHAPTER TWELVE

Thunder and Lightning

It was twelve blocks down Carrollton to the Nix Branch Library and twelve blocks back, but Fish walked the whole way. He was saving every penny for Liberty, and fourteen cents' bus fare bought a lot of Pard brand dog food. Just that morning, Mrs. Francis had said that a person could find about anything in a book, which was the reason for the long hike to the neighborhood library for the first time since he'd arrived in New Orleans.

"Pet training would be in the 600s." The librarian pointed Fish toward the far wall. "When you find what you want, bring it on up here and we'll get you signed up for a card," she said. Fish nodded, then step-clomped as quietly as he could across the hardwood floor. He'd been having a heck of a time getting Liberty used to her leash. Sometimes she tugged and pulled, as if it were a snake she needed to get away from. And sometimes she just plunked down and refused to move, as if Fish had hooked her up to a ship's anchor instead of a thin leather leash.

Fish perused the shelves. He had no idea there could be so many books on this one topic! He grabbed a couple and thumbed through them until he found a likely candidate. The librarian helped him fill out the form for the card and he was soon on his way. The book he picked suggested giving a treat each time the leash was used. That way, Liberty would associate it with something good. That made sense to Fish. If he'd known anything about dogs, he might have figured that out on his own.

The weather had turned when he stepped outside. Dark clouds scudded overhead and the air was so heavy he could've scooped it up and thrown it, like a snowball. He hadn't learned to read this sky yet, like he could the one back in Seattle, but he sure hoped it wasn't going to start raining before he got home. It'd ruin his library book. He paused under a drugstore awning, book open, waiting for traffic to clear so he could cross the street. *"The best training for man's best friend is kindness,"* the book said. *"Be patient and positive and you will soon have a well-mannered pooch."* Mo would appreciate that; she wasn't too happy at the holes Liberty had dug in the backyard.

When Fish looked up from the book, traffic had cleared. And there was Olympia walking with some friends. They were too far ahead to catch up to. Besides, he wasn't about to inflict himself with a gaggle of girls, so he hung back.

On the next block, he passed five or six white men, in rolled-up shirtsleeves, sitting on a row of wooden chairs outside a small store. One smoked a pipe, which reminded Fish of Pop; they all burst out laughing at something the pipe smoker said. Fish didn't hear what it was, but he couldn't help smiling, too. Another man, wearing a dark shirt, called out to the men as he crossed the street to join them. The pipe smoker swiveled on his seat to face his friend. The dark-shirted man reached one section of the banquette the same time as Olympia and her friends, only they were looking at something else and didn't see him. Didn't realize they were blocking his way. The next thing Fish knew, Olympia was on the ground, the man yelling horrible things at her. Her friends helped her to her feet, all the while tugging her off the banquette. The three of them stood in the street, at the curb, letting the man pass.

Fish tightened his grip on the library book. That man had shoved Olympia. Clean off the banquette. Out of pure meanness. And his pals on the chair kept laughing and talking like it was nothing out of the ordinary. Fish stared at them, trying to summon up the courage to say something. Do something.

Olympia and her friends hurried on. Fish hurried on, too, and not because of the changing weather. He crossed to the other side of the street, away from those men. The thick air and his shaky legs made the walk home seem to take forever.

When he let himself in the house, the notes of "All Creatures of our God and King" wobbled over the backyard fence from Miss Zona's house. Olympia practicing for church again. She missed a few notes. Fish wondered that she could play at all after what had happened.

He grabbed the leash and a piece of bologna from the icebox and went out to sit with Liberty in her pen under the live oak tree. He'd thrown it together that morning, using more scrap lumber and chicken wire from Mr. Campbell's. She barked a greeting, wiggling left and right like it was any other day, nudging his hand to scratch that hard-to-get spot above her tail.

"I missed you, too." Something about petting that sweet head, looking into those trusting eyes, helped to erase the ugliness he'd seen. "We're going to try an experiment, okay?" He broke the bologna into chunks and gave her one every time he clicked the leash on and off her collar. After about ten bites, he tried walking her around the yard. She seemed to forget she even had a leash on, trotting close to his hand, nosing it for more meat.

"I guess that works pretty good, huh, girl?" He gave her the last bite and sat under the live oak. She plunked down next to him, dozing off while he read more about dog training. Mo would be impressed if he could teach Liberty to fetch. She could get the paper or Mo's slippers; Mo would really go for that. She and Liberty would be best pals in no time.

Liberty twitched, sat up, and barked.

"What is it?" In the distance, Fish heard the rumble of thunder. "That won't hurt you." He tried to stroke her head. She tugged at the leash, dragging Fish in circles. "It's okay, girl. It's okay." He petted her until there weren't any more rumbles, and she settled. "I used to hate storms when I was a kid, too," he reassured her. "But it's okay. Mo says thunder is only God bowling." He rubbed the white patch on Liberty's chest. "But dogs probably don't know about God or bowling, do they?"

Mo was in a snit when she got home from work, so it didn't seem like the time to ask if Liberty could stay inside that night. Fish fell right to sleep after he went to bed but jerked awake when lightning lit up his window. He counted, one Mississippi, two Mississippi, three Mississippi . . . *crash!* That was close. He threw off the bedcovers and was outside as quickly as he could. He made out two shapes in the dark. One was wearing shorts and a light-colored top.

"Olympia?" He let himself into the pen. "What are you doing out here?"

"I heard Liberty crying." She had her arms tight around Liberty's neck. "She hates lightning."

"I think it's the thunder, but you're right. Storms scare her." He shivered as rain pelted his back. "Let's go in the shed."

He clipped on the leash and the three of them made their way inside, watching the fingers of lightning through the one window. Fish made a lap and Liberty curled up in it as best she could, trembling.

Fish stroked between her eyes; the book said that was calming to dogs.

The next lightning bolt turned the inside of the shed as bright as a summer day. In that flash, Fish saw the big bandage on Olympia's knee. Liberty shivered and he rubbed her all over, thinking. Should he say something to Olympia about what he'd seen?

"One Mississippi, two Mississippi, three Mississippi . . ." Olympia counted, and then *crash*.

Liberty shifted, tried to get up, but Fish kept petting her. Olympia reached over, too. "That's just God rearranging furniture." She comforted the dog. "Nothing to fret about."

"When I was little, I learned it was God bowling," Fish said.

Olympia laughed. "No, furniture. And the lightning flashes is the Almighty taking pictures of all His beautiful children." She shifted to sit cross-legged, too. "Ain't it funny the things our mothers tell us."

Fish was quiet a moment. "My mother never told me anything. She died when I was born."

Olympia clucked her tongue just like Miss Zona did sometimes. "That's rough."

He shrugged, watching drips run down the filthy shed window. "It's just the way it is."

Thunder clapped again and Liberty twitched. But she didn't try to get up.

"My mama got pneumonia when I was six. That's when I came to live with my grandmamma."

"Why didn't you live with your dad?"

Now Olympia shrugged. "Don't know where he is."

Liberty rolled onto her back, wedged between Fish and Olympia. They took turns rubbing her belly. Not talking, but easy.

"Sounds like the storm's dying down," Olympia said after a while.

"God must be done with the furniture." Fish smiled.

"I'm real sorry about that time I let her out."

Olympia concentrated on a spot by Liberty's white patch. "It was a sheer accident."

Fish nodded. "Sorry I got so mad."

"*Pfft.*" Olympia snorted. "You don't know the first thing about being mad. Wooie. You should see my auntie when she's fuming." She rested her head on her knees. "Grandmamma and the preacher say we have to turn the other cheek."

"Mo says you gotta stand up for yourself sometimes, too."

Olympia's voice got low. "It's different for us, Fish."

He stretched out his good leg. It was getting pins and needles in it from sitting so long. "You mean for kids?"

"I mean for us."

Fish thought about that man on the sidewalk. And the side-by-side water fountains labeled WHITE and COLORED. And about the invisible line in the streetcar that someone like him sat in front of and someone like Olympia sat in back of. "Mo says maybe the war will change that."

"Maybe." But she didn't sound near as convinced as Mo. They sat awhile longer, taking turns petting Liberty, until Olympia yawned. She got up and brushed off the seat of her shorts. "I better get back to bed. I think the storm's passed."

"I'm gonna stay with her a little while longer." Fish rubbed circles on Liberty's belly.

"You're a keeper, Fish," Olympia said. "Night."

He couldn't see her, but he imagined her padding through the darkened backyard and slipping through the hole in the fence and into Miss Zona's house.

Another flash of lightning caught Fish's eye. He counted but he got to twenty Mississippi and no thunder clapped. The storm was probably over, like Olympia said. He smiled to himself. Maybe that last flash *was* God taking a picture of one of His children.

Taking it of Olympia, one of his really nice ones.

CHAPTER THIRTEEN

Meeting the New Noah

Mo disappeared into the office, gently closing the door behind her. But that was no buffer for the words bellowed from within. "I'm a busy man! This isn't a kindergarten."

Fish tugged at the tie Mo had made him wear. He couldn't breathe.

The hollering continued, including a few choice bits that Fish would've gotten his mouth washed out for using. He edged away from the door, toward the exit.

A gaunt man glanced up from the papers scattered across his desk. "His bark is worse than his bite," he reassured Fish. Then he chuckled. "Generally."

Fish couldn't make out what Mo was saying, but from the lull in the volume, he knew she was saying something. This wasn't the first time he was grateful for his bulldog of a sister. Nothing much stopped her. Not even the hospital rules, back when he was on the polio ward. "He doesn't have a mother," she'd told the duty nurse who tried to enforce the parents-only visitation rule. "If he did, she'd be here. Now let me in." After that, no one said a word when Mo showed up to see Fish.

The blustering commenced again.

Mo might be able to tangle with a nun and win, but it was sounding like Mr. Higgins was getting the better of her. "I should probably go," Fish said aloud, to no one in particular.

"Take a load off." The gaunt man scooted back from his own desk and found Fish a chair. "I've got my money on your sis."

Before Fish could take advantage of the offered chair, the office door swung open and Mo stepped out. Bright spots of pink dotted her cheeks, but, otherwise, you wouldn't have a clue that she wasn't cool as a cucumber.

"Mr. Elliott," she said to Fish. "Mr. Higgins will see you now." Fish stood frozen in the center of the reception area. Mo made a little jerk with her head, signaling Fish to get a move on. He wiped one sweaty hand on his pants, and gripped a pad and pencil with the other.

"Don't worry," called the man. "He's had his shots!"

Fish took a deep breath and step-clomped through the doorway, into the office of Mr. Andrew Jackson Higgins. One of the most powerful men in America. A man who was such good friends with the president that FDR was planning to visit the factory in the fall.

The founder of Higgins Industries planted himself smack in the center of the room. He was taller than Pop; heftier, too. The crease in his trousers was sharp enough to slice bread and there wasn't a wrinkle in his white shirt. Fish had never seen such a fancy tie. And that tie clip had to be real gold.

Fish stuck out his hand as his father had taught

him. "Hello, sir." His mouth was so cottony, it sounded like he had a lisp. He licked his lips. Swallowed. "I'm Michael Elliott. But most people call me Fish."

Mr. Higgins's hand was as big as an armadillo and twice as rough. "Good to meet you, Fish. People call me Mr. Higgins." Mr. Higgins's breath carried more than a whiff of Old Grand-Dad whiskey. Mo had warned Fish about that.

Fish nodded.

Mr. Higgins laughed. "But I have a feeling we're going to be friends. And my friends call me A.J." He hadn't let go of Fish's hand and now tugged him over to a seat opposite an enormous desk. Some kind of intercom buzzed on his desk. "Hold up a minute, Fish. Gotta take this." He listened to a scratchy voice rasping from the machine, then barked back a series of orders. "Gosh darn it, Henry. I can't live with you and I can't live without you. Just do what I asked." Only, Mr. Higgins didn't say "gosh" and he didn't say "darn." He flipped a switch on the intercom and plopped himself in a leather swivel chair.

Fish nodded again. He began to feel a bit like that ventriloquist's dummy, Charlie McCarthy, with someone else controlling his body. He cleared his throat, set his notepad on his lap, and poised his pencil to take notes.

"I gotta tell you, Fish, I don't relish being someone's homework."

Fish blinked. Was Mr. Higgins going to change his mind after all? There went his assignment.

"But because it was you, I decided to make an exception." Mr. Higgins patted around his pocket, found a package of cigarettes, and pulled one out. His face softened. Was that pity in his eyes?

This was the one reaction Fish hated. More than any of the teasing. Someone feeling sorry for him because of the polio. Because of his leg. Fish tried to tuck it under the chair. Out of sight.

Mr. Higgins struck a match, ready to light the cigarette. Then he blew it out. "Guess your teacher would frown on that." He yanked open a desk drawer to toss the pack of cigarettes inside. He pulled out a cigar box. Fish's cigar box. "You might want this back," he said, sliding it across the desk. "I admire how you worked with what you had." He tugged on the ribbons. "Your girlfriend's probably missing these, however."

Fish felt the blood rush to his face. "She's my neighbor." Fish paused. "A girl who is my friend." At that moment, he realized the truth in that statement. Olympia was his friend.

Mr. Higgins smoothed his hand over his Brylcreemed hair. "I do the very thing myself. Make models. Sketch drawings." He leaned back, hands behind his head. "Sometimes, in school, when I was supposed to be doing something else."

Fish felt his face turn an even deeper shade of red. He did that, too.

Mr. Higgins chuckled. Then he stood up. "Come along with me, young man. I can't sit still for more than three minutes or I get cross-eyed." He headed toward the office door, motioning for Fish to follow. "See what I've built up here, why don't you?"

They stepped out into the reception area. Mo's eyebrow raised.

"Miss Elliott, hold my calls. I've got a VIP to escort around the plant."

Mr. Higgins barreled off. He didn't slow down for Fish, but Fish appreciated that. Being treated like a normal kid. He gave up on taking notes. It was too hard to keep pace with Mr. Higgins and write at the same time.

They left the office, zigzagging through the building until they were standing on a catwalk overlooking an enormous assembly room. A huge banner was draped across the far wall: THE MAN WHO RELAXES IS HELPING THE AXIS. Fish wondered if Mr. Higgins should update that sign. Most of the workers in the room below were not men but women in coveralls, their heads covered with kerchiefs.

"That's a lot of ships." Fish leaned over the rail to count. There must have been twenty-five LCVPs, each in a different stage of completion. He'd heard Mo talk about Mr. Higgins's assembly lines, but seeing them was another thing altogether. As each row of boats finished one step, it rolled forward for the next crew, the next part. The whole place looked like the ant farm he got for his birthday one year: No one and nothing was standing still.

Mr. Higgins rested against the railing. "They said I couldn't do it. But last year we delivered seven thousand LCVPs and a thousand LCMs. You get your sister to take you on a drive past Bayou St. John. It's cram-packed with ships waiting to be delivered to Uncle Sam." He clapped Fish on the back. "Two things I've learned, Fish." He held up a plump finger. "Don't let others set the bar for you." A second finger. "And if you think you can't, you're right."

From there, they strode on to the machine shop. Fish covered his ears; even Mr. Higgins didn't try to talk over the grinding and grating. They stopped by the woodshop and the rigging room. Fish was fascinated by the welders, with arcs of heat sparking from their tools. Think what he could build if he had his own soldering gun!

"Can you believe it? We'll put out forty-two LCMs this week alone." Even though he was the big boss and knew every detail of the company, Mr. Higgins sounded amazed. "Maybe next time I can take you on a little ride."

Fish had heard about Mr. Higgins's test drives. His favorite trick was to run a ship up Lake Pontchartrain's steep concrete seawall, scaring the bejeebies out of his passengers, then throw it into reverse to bump off. Fish was content to have gotten his ride from Roy.

They were about to enter another part of the plant, when a worried-looking man ran up to them. He and Mr. Higgins talked for a bit about steel and measurements and some other things Fish didn't track, and then Mr. Higgins said, "Gotta go, Fish. The Navy's trying to muck with my PT boat design. Big mistake." He poked at Fish's notebook. "Take this down: These Higgins boats are going to help win the war. Mark my word."

As he hurried away with the worried man, Mr. Higgins called over his shoulder, "I'd like to see that essay of yours when it's done!"

That thought had not even occurred to Fish. But he knew from Mo that when Mr. Higgins asked for something, you'd better deliver.

"And, finally, these words from Michael Elliott." Principal Sellars cleared his throat and read Fish's essay over the public address system. Fish kept his eyes on his desk, but sat taller in his chair. *"I will always remember Mr. Higgins's advice: If you think you can't, you're right. Because one thing a hero never does is give up. Mr. Higgins has inspired me to keep trying. He may not be a soldier, but he is a hero to me."*

The class broke into applause as Principal Sellars

finished reading. "Thank you, Lurelle, Daisy, and Michael for such fine work." The PA system crack- led off.

Mrs. Francis handed back the essays. Fish couldn't help admiring the A+ at the top of his paper. His first.

"Brownnoser." Wally kicked the back of Fish's chair. "I suppose you're going to stay after school and clean the blackboards, too."

"Actually, I'm not." Fish carefully placed his essay in his desk. "I've got to hurry home to take care of my dog."

|||||||||||||||||||||||||||||||||||||||||||||||||||||||||||||||||||||||||||||||||||||||||||||||

CHAPTER FOURTEEN

A Distant Shore

Erich found his sea legs quickly; some of the others, like Oskar, were green the entire voyage to New York. Erich gladly ate Oskar's portions, even if they were mostly cold C-rations. Erich could tell by his waistband that he had gained back several of the pounds lost while fighting in Africa.

"What do you think it will look like?" Erich wondered aloud as they rested on their bunks one night after supper. "New York?"

"Not like the postcards." Oskar shrugged. "The Luftwaffe bombed the Statue of Liberty."

"Wishful thinking," the Professor scoffed. "We've needed all our planes in Europe, in Africa." He polished his glasses with a dingy handkerchief, studying Erich. "Rest assured, we will be greeted by Lady Liberty."

Oskar made no comment but to heave into the bucket on the floor by his bunk.

Erich secretly hoped the Professor was right. They had been told so many things in the Army that had not proved true. As the three-week journey neared its end, Erich staked out a position on the rail each morning, one from which he would have a clear view of the harbor.

Shortly after breakfast on the twenty-first day, the ship slowed, turned toward the port, and there it was. The Statue of Liberty. In perfect condition. Though Erich could not read that famous poem from where he stood, he knew some of what it said: "Give me your tired, your poor, your huddled masses yearning to breathe free." That certainly seemed to describe this ship full of prisoners of war. Except for the most fervent of Nazis, the men were glad to be free of Hitler, free of the German Army.

The ship had barely docked at Ellis Island before the men were unloaded and marched into a long hall where they were stripped of their clothes and sprayed with a disinfectant. Erich was horrified to see dead lice fall from his hair like raindrops. Next they were led straight to shower stalls with rich soap, thick towels, and plenty of hot water. He scrubbed and scrubbed and scrubbed. When he stepped out, he was handed a duffel. He was astonished at what he found inside: four pairs of trousers, a belt, five shirts, socks, underwear, gloves, a jacket, a coat, a raincoat, a cap, and even a new pair of shoes. Nearby, they found cans of white paint and stencils. In bad German, a guard explained they were to paint each item of the new uniform with the letters *PW*.

"We're painting targets on ourselves," complained Oskar.

"Why would they bring us all this way to shoot us now?" From what Erich had seen so far, there would be more problems with the hard-core Nazis, always itching for a fight, than with the Americans.

Early the next morning, they were marched to a train station, where they boarded regular passenger cars, not the boxcars used to transport troops in Germany. Amazingly, a porter came through, offering sandwiches and hot coffee. "Sandwich, sir?" He stopped in front of Erich, smiling.

"*Danke*." Erich took roast beef.

Oskar refused food and drink the first time it was offered but not the second time. "I don't know what they're up to," he said, "but I'm hungry."

"Our captors have given me no reason to expect we will not be treated decently." The Professor took a calm sip of coffee.

"It's all for show," said Oskar. "Wait until they get us to the camps."

The two men bickered back and forth, but

their voices soon became background noise. Erich closed his eyes and drifted off.

The next time he awoke, they were pulling into a train station.

The sign said NEW ORLEANS.

CHAPTER FIFTEEN

"A Great Crusade"

Fish scraped bits of pancakes and bacon into Liberty's food dish. She gobbled them up, licking her muzzle before reaching around to lick her side. Miss Zona said her fur might not grow back over the wound, but that otherwise it was almost healed. Fish snapped on the leash to take her for their morning walk.

"Oh my gosh!" Mo's voice carried out the kitchen window. "Oh my gosh!" she repeated. Something in her tone gave Fish chills.

He hobbled up the porch stairs, Liberty at his heels. Mo didn't even say anything about no dogs in the house. Her hand was at her throat, her face white as the flour canister.

"Are you okay?" Fish looked around the kitchen. No sign of blood. "Is it Pop? Roy?" His heart pounded double time in his chest.

Mo's hands trembled as she cranked the knob to turn up the volume on the radio. "Listen."

The radio announcer's voice filled the room, smooth as cream. "At 7:32 a.m. Greenwich mean time, 2:32 a.m. Central war time, the Supreme Headquarters Allied Expeditionary Force launched its greatest overseas military operation. Allied armies are pouring ashore on the enemy-held soils of France, in one of the greatest amphibious attacks of the ages. Though we are not at liberty to give precise locations, we can say that General Eisenhower has called this action 'a great crusade.'"

"What does it mean?" Fish tightened his grip on Liberty's leash.

"I think it could mean the end of the war." Mo wiped her face with her apron. "And amphibious attacks. That means Higgins boats."

Mr. Higgins was right. His boats were going to win the war. "Do you think Pop was there? That he's okay?"

Mo sniffled, shook her head. "He'd be inland,

I'm sure. Building bridges for the troops and equipment." She wrapped Fish in a hug. "He'll be fine. Don't you worry."

Pop had seemed so far away all this time. His letters had been light, cheery. He talked about getting used to drinking tea, like the English, rather than coffee. And about the English fondness for cold toast. He wrote about the men in his unit, giving them all nicknames like Tex or Babyface or Stone. He'd never written about what he was actually doing, besides building bridges. He wasn't allowed to say where he was. And he certainly wouldn't tell them if he was in danger. Fish realized Pop's letters were the written version of his poker face. He'd never give anything away.

"At least Roy's not there," Fish said. "Do you think he's sorry about that?"

Mo made a sound that was a combination of a laugh and a sob. "Oh, Roy thinks he can win the war all by himself, no matter where he is, steering that ship of his." She glanced at the clock, then lifted her pocketbook from the chair back, where she'd left it hanging, and fished out a nickel. "There's still time before school. Go see if there's an extra edition of the *Times-Picayune*," she said. "The paper will have more information."

Miss Zona must have had the same idea, because he met up with Olympia on the street. Liberty trotted next to them, still not all that happy about being on leash. Mo said she was a gypsy dog. "She's too much like her name," Mo had teased.

Cali's Market had a slim stack of extras. Fish and Olympia turned over their nickels to Miss Rose. "Isn't it something?" Miss Rose straightened out the remaining newspapers in the stack. "I think the tide has finally turned." She gave them each a B.B. Bats taffy, saying, "Here's a lagniappe, something extra, to celebrate."

"Do you think your aunt saw any of the landings?" Fish unwrapped his B.B. Bat.

"I don't know." Olympia put her treat in her skirt pocket. "She doesn't write much about what she sees. Or what she does."

Fish licked his candy a few times. "That's like Pop. Roy, too."

"I don't think any of them are supposed to say what's really going on. Because of the censors," Olympia added. "But Grandmamma sent Auntie a diary so she could keep a record. For later. For after the war. Maybe we'll find out more then."

Car horns honked and pots and pans clanged around them as they walked home. New Orleans was celebrating the news. At least in their neighborhood. Fish had learned that his new hometown didn't need much of an excuse for a party or a parade.

The bells from the nearby Catholic church pealed the hour. "We better get a move on or we'll be late to school." Walking Liberty every day had built up his muscles. He could manage an awkward jog if he rocked his body from side to side. He and Olympia parted company at Miss Zona's front walk.

"See you after school!" she called.

At home, he wrapped up his taffy and stuck it on his dresser before grabbing his schoolbooks and lunch box. Then he situated Liberty in her pen. He refilled her water dish and scratched under her chin. "Be good. I'll be home before you know it."

She licked his hand, fixing him intently with her brown eyes.

"Don't even ask." He shook his head. "Mrs. Francis would not allow a dog at school."

There wasn't much attention paid to math or spelling or language arts that day. Mrs. Francis finally pulled down the big map hanging over the blackboard and they talked about where the Allied troops might have landed.

"My brother's a Marine," Wally reminded the class. "He could have been in the invasion."

"We will hold him in our thoughts," said

Mrs. Francis. "Along with all the other men and women in the Armed Services." Her eyes seemed bigger than usual behind those bifocals. But in a thoughtful, sad way.

At noon, Catholic churches all over town rang their bells for three solid minutes. The chiming traveled through Fish's ears, right into his bones. Instead of hearing *ding-dong*, he heard *Pop-Roy*. Over and over. He poked himself with the sharpened end of his pencil so he wouldn't cry. When the pealing faded away, Principal Sellars came over the public address system and led the students in a prayer for the success of the invasion. Wally's mind must have been on his brother. He didn't speak out of turn the rest of the day.

Fish thought hard about Roy and Pop all the way home, the darkening sky fitting his mood. If this were a movie, he'd find letters from them in the mailbox, telling him they were okay. But he lived in real life, not in a movie. The mailbox was empty.

Liberty sat up the minute she saw him, tail wagging. He hoped it wasn't just because he'd brought out a Milk-Bone.

"Only a few more days of school." His right leg caught on the wire of the gate as he dragged it through. "And then I can stay home every day."

Liberty nudged at his hand. "Hey, let's use some good manners." He motioned for her to sit. When she did, he broke off a chunk of the Milk-Bone. "Down." Another chunk of bone for a good down. "How about shake?" She hadn't mastered that one yet. As soon as Fish put his hand out to shake, she stuck her muzzle in it, looking for a treat. "Shake," he repeated. This time, she pawed at his right hand. Close enough. She got the last bite of Milk-Bone.

When she was done crunching, he attached her leash, let her out of the pen, and they started off for their afternoon walk. In the few weeks since catching Liberty, Fish had gotten to know more of their neighbors. People here liked to sit on their front porches or front stoops and watch the world go by. He waved to Mr. Pellegrini, who lived on the other side of Fig. If Mrs. Abellard was out, she usually had a treat for Liberty. A soupbone or pork chop scraps, and once, the last of a can of deviled ham. Mrs. Abellard's was one of Liberty's favorite stops. But she wasn't on her porch today.

Fish step-clomped along, with Liberty sniffing every other flower bush. He hollered "hey" to the Beasley sisters, both with their hair up in rollers. "We're headed to the D-day prayer service tonight," called out Miss Marvelle Beasley.

"Might we see you there?" added Miss Jewell Beasley.

"Homework!" Fish answered with a tiny white lie. The last week of school, even Mrs. Francis gave up on homework. The Beasley sisters might go to church at least three times a week, but Fish was content with attending on Christmas and Easter.

"Another time, then," called Miss Marvelle.

Fish nodded. He and Liberty neared the spot

where they usually turned around to head back. Being a Southern dog, Liberty didn't seem much affected by the heat and humidity. But sweat ran down Fish's back, and there was a cold Barq's root beer calling him from the icebox. Plus, he still had his exercises to do. He thought his knee was bending a little bit more and his right leg didn't seem that much shorter than his left anymore. But he didn't know if it was because of the bike riding or his contraption, so he kept up with both.

Some movement across the way caught his eye. A Western Union delivery boy pedaled up to the DeSotos'. He dismounted his bike, straightened his jacket, and climbed up the front porch steps. A Blue Star Flag, for the DeSotos' only son, hung next to the front door. The telegram boy moved heavily, slowly, then stood on the porch, hand poised to knock, but not knocking for several moments. Finally, knuckles rapped on wood and, moments later, the door opened. The telegram boy handed Mrs. DeSoto an envelope.

Fish had never heard such a noise before. Not even in the wards when kids were in excruciating pain. He hoped he'd never hear anything like it again. Mrs. DeSoto fell, sobbing, against the doorframe. The delivery boy looked around, hollering, "Help. Anybody? Help!"

The Beasley sisters shuffled across the street, hair rollers bobbing on their gray heads. They caught Mrs. DeSoto up in their arms and helped her into the house.

Fish swallowed hard, then tugged on Liberty's leash. "Let's go home."

The next day, when they took their afternoon walk, the blue star in the DeSotos' service flag was replaced with a gold one. A gold star for a life lost.

CHAPTER SIXTEEN

Now You See Her, Now You Don't

Mo didn't like leaving Fish on his own so much. She'd offered to sign him up for some classes at the YMCA. But Fish had managed to dodge that bullet. He didn't really have time anyway. He was busy with Liberty and Olympia. The Three Musketeers, the Beasley sisters called them, watching from their front porch, always ready with lemonade and dog biscuits. Sometimes Fish and Olympia helped Mrs. DeSoto in her Victory Garden, and Mr. Campbell was happy to put them to work sorting nails and screws at his store.

For one whole week, Olympia had Bible School at her church. By the last day, Fish was tired of his new library book and his latest project: a lazy Susan for Miss Zona's kitchen table. He was tired of being cooped up at home.

"Want to go for a walk, girl?" Liberty perked up at the word, waggling her hind end. Fish got her leash and they set off. Miss Zona didn't allow Olympia to wander outside their neighborhood, so Fish decided he and Liberty would go on an adventure. Wander and explore. They meandered up this street and that, dodging from one shady spot to the next, until they found themselves at the New Basin Canal. Wally, Ernie, and some other boys from school were stripped to their skivvies, splashing in the murky water.

Fish leaned in the shade of a live oak, watching their game. It didn't seem to have any rules but involved taking turns throwing milk caps into the canal and jumping in after them. On Wally's next turn, he cannonballed, hooting and hollering the whole time. When he broke through the surface, he put up his fists like a prizefighter.

"I'm the champion!" he crowed. "Nobody can beat me."

It was hotter than hot and, even dirty, the canal water looked inviting. Cool. Fish tied Liberty's leash around a nearby tree. "Can I try?" He hobbled over to the group.

"You?" Wally snorted.

"Yeah." Fish kicked off his sneakers. "You chicken?"

Ernie grinned and grabbed another handful of milk caps, ready to toss them in.

"Race ya," Wally hollered.

Fish stepped to the edge of the canal, peeling off his shirt, poised for action.

"On the count of three!" Ernie called. "One, two —"

Wally jumped. Fish dived right after. In the water, there was no such thing as a bad leg. Nurse Meg had called him her fish. Mo got such a kick out of that, the name stuck. It didn't matter to Fish that this canal was dirty and cold. Any water gave him wings.

He cleanly stroked to where he'd seen the cap go in, dived, and snatched it up.

"Beginner's luck," Wally sputtered. They went again. Fish beat him two more times.

"So you're a swimmer and an egghead," Wally said. But he grinned and stuck out his hand, to show no hard feelings. Shivering and smelling worse than wet dogs, the boys spread out along the canal, drying in the sun. Ernie gave Fish a swig of his orange Nehi and Wally shared the brown ones from a roll of Necco Wafers. Liberty lolled on her back, taking belly rubs from all the boys. When the church bells chimed five, Wally gathered up his things. "Time for supper."

The rest of the boys fanned out toward their homes.

"See you around, Fish," said Ernie.

"See you around," Fish answered. He got home in such a good mood, he ate two helpings of Mo's latest Meatless Tuesday creation.

The next morning, Mo poured herself a cup of coffee. "If you finish those letters before I leave, I can mail them from work."

Fish marveled that she could drink something hot with the air already thick as oatmeal. He spooned up some cornflakes, then wrote another line in the letter to Pop. *"I've taught Liberty* sit *and* down. *We're working on* shake, *too."* He glanced at the picture he'd drawn of his dog, right at the top of the page. He wasn't much of an artist, but Pop would get the general idea. *"She's a good dog, Pop. You're going to love her. Take care of yourself."* He signed off *"Forward, Fish,"* then quickly added a few sentences to Roy's letter. *"I would like an aloha shirt,"* he replied to Roy's question. *"Could you get something for Olympia, too? I'll pay you back."* Roy's unit had finished training in San Diego and was now in Honolulu for some R&R before their next assignment. *"How about a grass skirt?"* he wrote. *"Don't worry, I am taking care of Mo, like you asked. Well, as best as I can. You know how she is.*" He signed off that letter, too, folded each one into an envelope, licked them shut, and pasted on stamps. He handed the envelopes to his sister.

"What's on your agenda today?" Mo faced the mirror near the back door, situated her hat on her head, then rubbed a bit of lipstick off her front tooth.

"Weeding Miss Zona's Victory Garden." Fish spooned up the last of the cornflakes.

"Can you also make time to give Liberty a bath?" Mo grabbed her pocketbook. "I think she's still got fleas. See you tonight, kiddo." She blew Fish a kiss and hurried off to the streetcar.

Fish washed up the breakfast dishes, then whistled for Liberty. He got her out of her pen and clicked the leash onto her collar. She followed him through the gap in the fence over to Miss Zona's backyard. She made herself at home under the Indian Hawthorn bush; Fish tied the leash to a branch. His trap had finally snagged that hungry rabbit. Fish and Olympia relocated it to the big woods by the railroad tracks. Now, instead of critter problems, Miss Zona had weeds. And she paid them a nickel for each bucketful.

"Hey, y'all!" Olympia bounced down the stairs. Liberty wagged her tail in greeting but didn't move from her spot in the cool earth. Olympia ran to her, fussing like she hadn't seen Liberty in weeks.

"Are you going to help?" Fish dumped his first bucket of weeds in the burn barrel.

Olympia stuck out her tongue at Fish. "I'm not finished loving on Liberty."

Another few minutes went by. Fish threw a dirt clod at Olympia. She ignored him and began rubbing Liberty's belly.

"Mmm, mmm, that snowball sure is going to taste good." Fish made a big deal of smacking his lips. "Too bad you won't get one. Because I'm doing all the work."

"You sound like the Little Red Hen from my storybook." Olympia pressed the back of her hand to her forehead. "I have to plant the wheat and mill the flour and bake the bread all by myself," she carried on.

Fish had to laugh. "Well, it would go quicker if you helped."

She gave Liberty one last pat, then joined Fish in the garden. She was quicker than he was, so she caught right up. They both looked like they'd run through a sprinkler by the time they'd each filled three buckets.

"I could probably get used to the heat," Fish said. "But why does it always have to be so sticky?" He brushed his sweaty hair off his forehead.

"Keeps most of the Yankees away." Olympia cackled. " 'Cept you."

Fish threw another handful of weeds at her. She threw some right back.

"You children working out there?" Miss Zona called from the kitchen. "Because from where I sit, it looks like a good deal of horsing around."

"We're almost done, Grandmamma!" Olympia

picked up the scattered weeds. Fish helped. They surveyed the garden.

"I think we got them all." Fish pulled one tiny weed from underneath a tomato plant.

"Let's go get that snowball," Olympia said. "I'm about to melt."

They collected their wages from Miss Zona, who carefully removed the coins from a Lipton tea tin in the cupboard. Liberty panted, tongue hanging out, as she trotted along behind to the snowball shop. Olympia was partial to peach; Fish ordered grape. They plopped onto a bench — Liberty took shelter underneath — in the corner park, scooping the finely shaved flavored ice with wooden spoons. Fish hated the feel of the wood on his tongue, so he dropped the icy mix into his mouth. From time to time, he dropped a spoonful into his hand and let Liberty lap it up. Fish leaned his head against the back of the bench, feeling the icy cold trickle down his throat. Maybe he could invent something like a snowball to cool off the outside of a body. Something better than an electric fan.

Fish lifted his head at the clip-clop of horse hooves.

"Watermelons. Red to the rind. Watermelons. Red to the rind." The watermelon man flicked the reins, urging on the old horse that was pulling a small wagon filled with green ovals. "Watermelons!"

"White horse!" Olympia nudged Fish. "You can make a wish. But quick." She squinched her eyes shut.

Liberty nudged Fish's hand for another bite of snowball. He obliged. Then he closed his own eyes and wished, too.

The horse and driver clip-clopped over to a nearby row of shade trees. The driver hopped down, brought out a bucket of water, and let the horse drink. Then he poured some of the water on the horse's back to cool it off. The horse looked pretty happy about that, shaking itself and whinnying.

"I'm not going to tell you what I wished for," Olympia announced. "Otherwise it won't come true."

Fish shrugged. Everybody knew that rule.

"Okay. I'll tell you this much. It has to do with my auntie."

Fish reminded himself never to tell Olympia a secret. She wouldn't be able to keep it for more than three seconds. He imagined their wishes were pretty much the same: Olympia wishing her aunt back home safe, and him wishing the same for Pop and Roy. Safe and soon.

The D-day invasion didn't end the war straight off as Mo had thought it might, although things were going the Allies' way. Right before the Fourth of July, Allied troops had liberated Cherbourg, France. But there were still Nazis to fight in Europe. And the Japanese in the Pacific. Now Mo said maybe by Christmas it would all be over.

Fish let Liberty lap up the last of the syrup in the bottom of the snowball cup. Watching that horse had reminded him. "Want to help give her a bath?"

He was afraid Mo was right about Liberty's fleas. He'd found another bite on his leg that morning. Just thinking about it made him itch.

Olympia jumped off the bench. "Sure."

They pitched their trash and walked slowly home under a darkening sky. Each afternoon that week, clouds had scudded in, bringing thunderstorms. Fish did everything he could to comfort Liberty. Even moved her to the shed, though she fretted about being shut up, so she wouldn't be under the tree, in case of lightning strikes. But no amount of pleading would convince Mo to let her in the house. As long as there was one flea on her fur, Liberty was an outside dog only.

Fish peeled off his shirt and dragged the hose over to the old bathtub. When it was full enough, he undid Liberty's collar and coaxed her in with a Milk-Bone. She stood there, up to her knees in water. She didn't try to get out, but her eyes said, *Do I have to?*

Olympia lathered up some soap in her hands and rubbed it over Liberty's back. "That gash healed up real nice," she said. "The way the fur grew back over it, you don't hardly see anything."

Fish worked on Liberty's legs, getting those stockings of hers as white as he could.

Far in the distance, he heard a gentle rumble.

"We better hurry," Olympia said. "Another storm's on its way."

Fish picked up the hose and began rinsing off the soap. Liberty was at the end of her patience and shook herself, head to toe. Olympia backed off, laughing.

"Wait a sec!" Fish said. "Stay!" Liberty kept shaking.

"Turn off the hose, brainless!" Olympia laughed. "She's going to drown me." She swiped at her wet face.

Fish stepped over to the faucet and turned it to the right. At that moment, the storm no longer threatened. It arrived like a train roaring down the tracks.

Liberty shivered for a second.

And then, slippery and wet, she ran.

"Liberty!" He hobbled after her. "Here, girl, here!"

Olympia tore off across the yard. "There's nothing to grab on to!" She picked up her pace. "You took off her collar!" Her bare feet slapped the ground, one-two-one-two-one-two. But Liberty zipped out of reach.

"Li-ber-ty!" Fish screamed her name.

They chased her for blocks. But she put too much distance between them. They couldn't catch up.

She was gone.

CHAPTER SEVENTEEN

Eighty Cents a Day

The first days at Camp Plauche stretched out like years. Oskar was content to read books from the camp library and the Professor took university classes. Philosophy! Geology! Modern literature! Erich signed up for the English classes; those, he could see a purpose in. But that was all he could see purpose in. There were the soccer games, to be sure, but he didn't play. He kept to himself. Not even the Professor, with his kindly ways, could draw him out in conversation.

When the guards asked for day laborers, Erich raised his hand. At first, the jobs were confined to the camp. Mending the chain-link fence. Filling in potholes. Painting barracks. All tedious but with each one was some task that could be accomplished by a solitary person. And Erich always offered to do that solitary task. Anything to be as alone as he felt.

The POWs were paid their wages of eighty cents a day in scrip, tickets they could redeem for Cokes and writing paper and smokes. No cash, for fear it might be used in an escape. No one had tried, yet, from this camp. But there had been rumors of escapes from other camps.

Erich had noticed these stateside guards were just as eager as those in Algiers for "Nazi" souvenirs. At first, he'd made gifts of the little birds he carved. The downy woodpecker was a special hit. He was now quite grateful to his grandfather for passing on his wood-carving skills. Sergeant Tucker was a new father, so Erich carved a little boy figure and traded it for a five-dollar bill. "A souvenir," Erich told Sergeant Tucker. "A souvenir of my time as a guest of the United States."

Americans were so trusting.

CHAPTER EIGHTEEN

Big Brass and Big Bullies

Olympia sat on Fish's back porch, kicking her heels against the stair riser. "She loves you. She only ran because she was scared."

Fish held his chin in his hands. It didn't much matter why Liberty was gone. She was gone. Had been gone for a week. "Mo says she'll come back when she's hungry enough." He'd refilled the pie tin dog dish with corn bread and syrup and ham scraps from breakfast.

Olympia's braids bounced around as she nodded. "'Course she will."

Mo poked her head out the back door. "You two about ready? Mr. Haddock will be here soon."

He stood up, brushed off the seat of his pants. Olympia fluffed out the skirt of her dress.

"You're sure this is okay?" she asked Mo.

Her question took Fish back to that day coming home from the library. He caught Mo's eye. Mr. Haddock wouldn't treat Olympia the way that man had, would he?

"Mr. Haddock is a gentleman," Mo assured Olympia. "And very forward thinking." She fluffed her hair a bit. "Though he is an exceptionally slow driver."

Mr. Higgins was throwing a big celebration out at Lake Pontchartrain in honor of the shipyard's ten thousandth ship. Mo had three grandstand passes; Fish invited Olympia. After all, she had walked the neighborhood with him, going door to door to see if anyone had caught sight of a little brown cur hound. The only house they'd bypassed was Mr. LaVache's. It was unanimous that they'd best not bother him about Liberty.

Fish had wanted to wear the aloha shirt Roy sent. But Mo nixed that. "Not when you're in the viewing party," she said. So he'd put on a plain old button-down instead. He could already feel sweat rivulets running down his back as they walked. The aloha shirt would've been cooler. "It looks like it won't rain," he observed.

Mo laughed. "Mr. Higgins would not permit it. Not today."

Mr. Haddock's sedan pulled up to the curb and they climbed in, Mo in front, Fish and Olympia in back. Mr. Haddock was a poky slow driver, like Mo had said, but riding in a car was a nice treat. Besides, Fish didn't know what he would've done on the streetcar. He couldn't let Olympia sit in the back by herself. And he would've gotten plenty of dirty looks if he'd joined her.

"The boss has all kinds of brass lined up for the day," Mo said. "Brace yourself for lots of speeches."

Fish and Olympia exchanged glances. If it got too boring, they could go in search of some ice cream.

Finally, Mr. Haddock parked the car and they were soon hiking toward the seawall with hundreds of other New Orleanians, each as proud of

Mr. Higgins and his ships as if they worked at the shipyard themselves. Newspaper reporters and photographers meandered through the crowd, getting shots before the big celebration.

"Mr. Haddock! Miss Elliott!" One of the younger engineers in the office caught sight of them and flagged them to their spots on the seawall. "Will you look at all the people?" he asked, after giving Mo a hand up.

"Well, our boss makes this town pretty proud." Mo straightened her hat, gone askew during the step up.

Olympia stood very close to Fish. She hadn't said a word since they got into Mr. Haddock's car. Fish looked around at the crowd. Nearly all the faces were white, like his. He punched Olympia in the arm to let her know she was okay here. Safe. Distracted by thinking about her, he almost missed sighting Mr. Higgins, gleaming in a white seersucker suit and hat. Would he give a speech, too? Fish waved, but Mr. Higgins probably couldn't even pick him out of the crowd, there were that many people.

Mo had been right. There were lots of "brass," and lots of speeches. Boring speeches. Fish's legs grew tired, even his good leg. Mo had said the grand finale of the afternoon would be a demonstration with real troops performing a mock landing on the beach. He nudged Olympia again. "Want to go walk around?"

She shrugged.

Mo overheard. "Don't go too far," she cautioned. "And stay together. I don't want to lose either of you in this crowd." She reached for her pocketbook. "Do you need some spending money?"

Fish patted his pocket. He still had some coins from weeding for Miss Zona.

As soon as he and Olympia wiggled down from their viewing spots, others filled right in. They made their way down a grassy slope to a large open area where a handful of Army trucks were parked. Soldiers in full gear spilled out of the trucks. Fish could only imagine how hot they were, in helmets and uniforms, carrying packs and guns. Though it was only for show, each man wore a determined expression, as if there was no difference between this beach and the beaches at Normandy or on some Pacific island.

"Watch out there, kids." A solider ran by, leading a single file of his comrades, guns swinging in their arms as they ran. Fish and Olympia stepped aside, letting them pass.

"Their LCVPs must be over that way," Fish said. "Want to go? We can see how they get in."

"I need to find the ladies' first." Olympia looked in the opposite direction. "You can wait here if you want."

Fish remembered Mo's warning. "Naw. I better come along."

"I'll be quick," she said. "I promise."

They made their way to the right restroom. Fish paced at the fringes. A couple of men sat at a table nearby, drinking beer, talking really loud and waving their arms around. Fish was going to move away from them, when he realized that one of the men looked familiar. It was that old grouch, Mr. LaVache. Before Fish could step back, he heard something that made him feel like he had shaved ice flowing through his veins, not blood.

He moved closer still.

"I tell you, LaVache, if those are hound pups, you could make yourself some nice money," the friend said.

"How long do you think I gotta wait, Pie?" Mr. LaVache swigged at his beer.

"I can tell before their eyes even open," the man, Pie, bragged. "If they're mutts, you can just drown 'em. By the looks of her, it's only another month."

Mr. LaVache spit. "Well, I better get something out of those pups if I have to feed her for a month."

"I sold my last litter for a hundred bucks a pup." Pie opened another bottle. "'Course, everyone wants a Pie DuFour dog, if I do say so myself." He burped. "With that dog, you don't know how she hunts, so maybe only seventy-five dollars. But if she has a litter of five or six, that's —" He took a drink. "Gotta be close to three hundred."

Fish shook his head. It'd be closer to four hundred. Mr. LaVache's friend was dumb and creepy. This conversation was making him sick. Fish started to back away again.

"I heard those two kids were looking for the dog, too. Those Beasley biddies told me." LaVache snorted. "Figures that the only friend that crippled kid would have would be a girl like her."

Fish felt his limbs turn wooden. They were talking about him and Olympia! Did that mean the dog they were talking about was —

"There you are." Olympia skipped up to him. "What's wrong?"

"Mo's going to kill me, but I have to leave." He started toward the streetcar stop.

He had to get home. Now.

"Wait up!" Olympia ran after him. "I'm coming, too."

CHAPTER NINETEEN

‖‖

Friedrich's Twin

Erich did not think much of this latest farmer they were working for. Others had at least offered water to supplement what the Army provided for their noon dinner. Some families even offered cakes and cookies. And those delicious sweets called pralines. But not LaVache. Erich could imagine him in some long-ago time, cracking a whip against the back of a burdened slave.

Among other tasks, the POWs had been hired to repair his chicken coops, which needed tearing down, not repair. But what was it to Erich? He took the task of sawing the lengths of siding. That was something he could do by himself. He set up a station under one of the few trees. How did people survive in this heat? Sometimes the air was so heavy that Erich could scarcely breathe. He took care to make his canteen last the entire workday. Around four, Sergeant Tucker motioned the POWs back into the trucks for the return to camp. From the sounds of things, they were to come back again. Erich didn't mind. LaVache aside, this job had been all right. Away from the camp. Out of doors. And working around chickens made him feel right at home. Erich wondered how Mutti's had fared with the war. He supposed that her flock had gone, one by one, to the supper table.

He was the last to hop into the back of the truck, holding on to the side as Tucker gunned the engine and left LaVache behind. A boy walking down the street caught Erich's attention. Walking wasn't quite the right word. The boy hobbled along with an uneven gait. Erich shivered, stared. Then shook his head. Of course it wasn't Friedrich. His brother was thousands of miles away. But that boy could be his twin.

Erich could not look away, could not stop staring. He kept watching until the boy was a mere speck in the distance.

CHAPTER TWENTY

Caged

Fish was right. Mo was furious. Even though he and Olympia had left a note on Mr. Haddock's windshield, saying that they'd gone home.

He could almost see steam coming out her ears. "I don't care what the reason was." She'd held up her hand and wouldn't even let Fish explain. "You didn't have permission to leave. And I wasted a lot of Mr. Haddock's time looking for you." She'd sent Fish to his room and sent Olympia home for Miss Zona to deal with.

He hadn't meant to upset Mo. But it had been a matter of life and death. He and Olympia caught the first streetcar home — it was empty enough that they could sit together near the middle — and went straight to Mr. LaVache's house. His truck wasn't in the driveway; he and Pie DuFour must've driven it to the beach. Still, Fish felt Mr. LaVache's slimy presence as they approached his place from the back. It made him glance over his shoulder every other step. At first, all they saw was the garden and the chicken coops. Looked like he was doing some repairs to some of them. Then Fish saw it. A pen, a cage really, with Liberty chained to a stake inside.

"How did he get her?" Olympia's words came out like a sob.

Fish shook his head. She'd probably gotten hungry enough, being gone so long, to take food from anybody. And she looked like she was eating well, even gained weight. They eased closer, checking everything out. It didn't appear they could be seen from the street, thanks to an overgrown prickly shrub. Of course Mr. LaVache would plant something with prickers.

The moment she saw them, Liberty tugged at the chain, straining to get close to the fence, closer to Fish. But the chain, twisted around the stake, caught her up short. She whined.

"That's like to break my heart." Olympia grabbed Fish's arm. "We've got to get her out."

"You keep watch and I'll undo the latch." He crept forward as smoothly as he could manage, until he was just about on the pen. Then he got to feeling sick all over again.

A huge padlock held the gate shut. It looked like it weighed more than Olympia, it was that sturdy. Fish tugged and tugged, but it didn't budge. He slapped it in his frustration, setting it swinging back and forth, with a taunting scrape of metal on metal.

"What are you waiting for?" Olympia stage-whispered from behind one of the henhouses. She couldn't see the lock from her vantage point. "Aren't you going to let her out?"

"He's latched her up, good and tight."

Olympia moved closer to see for herself. "That is one ugly man. Who would do that to a dog?"

Fish started to shake his head, then he made sense of the rest of Mr. LaVache's conversation with his drinking buddy. "Puppies." He stared through the mesh at Liberty, pressing his forehead against the warm metal. She was fatter because she was going to have puppies. He told Olympia what he'd overheard. Most of it, anyway. He couldn't bear to say the part about the plans for the puppies.

"Could we tell the police?" Olympia suggested.

"How would I prove she's my dog?" Fish asked. "It'd be my word against his."

Olympia's eyes darted around the yard as if she might see something there that would answer their problem. "Well, what about Mo? She's a spark plug. Or wait." Olympia flapped her hands. "What about that Mr. Higgins? He knows everybody in town."

Fish tried to force his hand through the mesh in the fence, tried to pet Liberty, to comfort her. His hand was too big. "I don't think even Mr. Higgins can fix this problem."

"Well, what are you going to do?" Olympia's skinny arm could fit through, but it wasn't long enough to reach Liberty. "It's okay, girl."

He kicked at the cage with his left leg. Stupid thing looked solid, not like the pen he'd built at home. "I don't know." He held his hand up to the mesh, and Liberty strained to meet it. "But I'm going to do something, that's for sure."

A trip to the library uncovered another book on dogs. "It says it takes around sixty-three days for the puppies to come," Fish reported back to Olympia. He figured that Liberty got pregnant during the time she'd run away, after the storm. "That means she'll have them around the third week in September."

"I can't believe he was that rude to your sister." Olympia peeled the banana she'd brought over and handed half to Fish.

"I know." Fish took a bite, and swallowed. Mo hadn't been happy about going to talk to Mr. LaVache at first, but when she saw for herself how he was keeping Liberty chained up, she boiled over like a percolator.

"What kind of man are you, keeping an animal restrained like that? In this heat?" Mo wouldn't back off the porch, even when Mr. LaVache tried to close the door in her face. "My brother was caring for this dog. She doesn't belong to you. Let him have her back."

But Mo's arguments got them nowhere. Mr. LaVache had told them to get off his property and if they came back, he'd call the sheriff.

"So we have some time to make a plan." Olympia pulled at a banana string. "Can't you invent some gizmo to cut through that lock?"

"I don't need to invent a gizmo," he said. "A hacksaw would do it. But it would take forever. He'd catch us for sure."

Olympia took a bite, chewing. "Maybe we could let the air out of his truck tires?"

Fish looked at her. "How would that help?"

"I dunno." She shrugged. "I just saw it in a movie a while back."

He finished off his chunk of banana. "Until we think of something, I'm going to go every day and take her some food. Let her know I haven't forgotten her."

"I'll come along," Olympia said.

Fish nodded.

Her elbow tapped him in the side. "You'll think of something. I know you will."

He appreciated the vote of confidence. He wished he believed it himself. But he was just a kid. A kid with a bad leg. What could he do?

CHAPTER TWENTY-ONE

||||||||||||||||||||||||||||||||||||||||||||||||||||||||||||||||||||||||||||||||||||||

Der Hund

LaVache should raise swine, not chickens. He would be right at home with them. No, that was an insult to pigs. The way he kept that dog, chained up all day. And any fool could tell she was pregnant. Erich spat into the dirt, watching dust rise behind the saliva, to get the taste of that man out of his mouth. He was not going to be on the truck the next time it came to this place. He'd dealt with enough tyrants in the army.

The big red hen pecked around Erich's feet as he finished nailing new treads to the ramp. Bossy old thing: It was almost as if she was telling him to hurry up. He could see why she was impatient; the old ramp had nearly rotted through. These hens had to be part tightrope artists to bed down in the coops at night. Erich briefly fantasized about whacking LaVache over the head with the new ramp. He deserved no better.

Erich managed to resist the temptation, carrying the ramp over to the coop to nail it in place. Then he stood, swiping at the sweat on his forehead. He had the sense of being watched. He slowly swiveled to look over his shoulder.

That pale-skinned limping boy. He stood at the edge of LaVache's property, holding a paper sack. Watching. He had company this time. A wiry, dark girl waited with him, hands on her skinny hips. Erich smiled, waved. The girl waved back, her braids bouncing with the energy of her motions. The boy may have nodded. Erich wasn't sure.

The two children put their heads together, conferring. The sack traded hands. With a quick glance left and right, the girl ran straight to

Erich, handing it to him. "For Liberty," she said. "For the dog." Those last words were louder, as if she thought he could understand English better at high volume.

"Ah. *Der Hund*." He took the sack. "The dog. She needs a friend."

From near the house, LaVache began bellowing about something. The girl flew back to the boy.

Erich faced the children, gave them the thumbs-up sign. Then, dodging around the back side of the coops, away from the odious LaVache, he tossed the contents of the sack – a hot dog and bun and a warm slice of that oddly yellow cheese the Americans seemed to love – through the chain links to the hungry dog. She devoured it, fixing grateful eyes on Erich. He looked to the back of the acreage again. There was no sign of the children.

The dog pressed her nose against the wire

fencing of her pen, trying to lick Erich's hand. He did his best to rub her muzzle through the mesh. She sighed.

Perhaps he would come back to work for LaVache after all.

CHAPTER TWENTY-TWO

Friend or Foe?

Fish clipped a newspaper headline to take to school for current events: BEACH BATTLE AT ANGAUR. He brought a map along to show where the tiny island was, way out in the middle of the Pacific, south of Guam, east of the Philippines. How did the Marines and the Navy even find these places? How did the Japanese? All that commotion for tiny specks in that expanse of blue. But Miss Devereux was big on current events. "Your grandchildren will want to know about these times," she said. "And if you don't tell them, who will?" Fish couldn't picture himself as a grandfather, but if Miss Devereux said something, they all believed it. She was as pretty as Deanna Durbin and as sweet as Miss Zona's fudge. Fish caught Wally leaving an apple on her desk when he thought no one was looking.

Sixth grade held some nice surprises, aside from Miss Devereux. It wasn't until Mo took him shopping for new chinos to wear to school that Fish realized he'd grown over the summer. And she didn't have to hem his right pant leg up as much as usual. Could be that all that bike riding and walking to feed Liberty were paying off. And only a couple of weeks into the school year, Fish had been picked to be on a dodgeball team at recess. Twice. Working in Miss Zona's garden had improved his throwing arm.

All that good didn't make up for the painful. Mr. LaVache still had Liberty. Fish checked on her every day. Despite Olympia's faith in him, he hadn't figured out how to rescue her. Liberty seemed in decent health, no thanks to Mr. LaVache. Fish didn't know what he fed her, but she gobbled down every scrap he and Olympia brought. It was harder to get close to her now, too, with all those POWs working on the farm. But that one seemed to have a soft spot for dogs. Fish hadn't wanted to trust him. But Olympia talked him into it.

"He doesn't look much older than my cousin in high school," Olympia had said after she approached the POW the first time. After that, he seemed to be watching for them and always found an excuse to wander to the back of the property to get whatever food they'd brought for Liberty. *Hund*. That's what he called her. Once he had called Fish Friedrich. Fish wasn't sure what that meant. He hoped it didn't mean "crippled kid."

"Don't forget the spelling test tomorrow," Miss Devereux reminded Fish and his classmates as they scuffed out of the classroom at the end of the day.

Lurelle fell into step with Fish. "You did a real nice job with your current events, Fish." She fussed with the bow in her hair. "I can hardly read the papers sometimes, thinking about my big brother over there fighting. Seems like all I see is the bad news."

Fish nodded. On Friday, Mo had gotten teary after reading the front page. Fish guessed what had upset her: an article reporting the number of US casualties so far in the war. Almost 400,000. It didn't help that it had been forever since they'd heard from Roy.

"Well, see you tomorrow." Lurelle hurried off to meet her girlfriends, who were giggling together out in the hall.

Fish started home. He'd be on his own today to carry food to Liberty because Olympia had to practice for a solo over at their church. After the chicken farm, he'd finish those letters to Pop and Roy. Pop had finally received the Voice-O-Graph. He'd written back that one of his buddies had a record player and that the whole tent had listened to it. *"It made it seem as if you were right here, Fish,"* Pop had written. *"Sure brightened up this rainy day."* Those words made Fish feel pretty great. As if his being right there was something Pop really wanted. Even with his leg the way it was.

From the icebox, Fish grabbed the scraps he'd saved, including part of a peanut butter sandwich, a slice of Velveeta, and some red beans and rice. And some green beans, because Liberty seemed to like them as much as Roy did. Fish wrapped everything in tinfoil and started off for Mr. LaVache's.

The Army truck was parked on the street out front, which meant POWs. Fish had heard that they got paid something like ten cents a day doing work around the parish. But that they couldn't earn cash money in case they tried to use it to escape. They got paid in tickets or something like that. It would take more than ten cents' worth of tickets to make Fish want to work for *that* man. But maybe the POWs didn't have a choice. The more he thought about it, the more he was sure they didn't have a choice. Who would choose to work for Mr. LaVache?

Approaching from the back, as he usually did, Fish saw "their" POW. He nodded when he spotted Fish but held his hand up. Fish stopped. He could hear Mr. LaVache hollering and carrying on. The POW disappeared around the corner of one of the chicken coops. Then a truck door slammed and an engine clattered to life. Shortly after that, the POW came back. He walked right up to Fish and spoke to him for the first time.

"He's gone to get more lumber." His English was almost perfect. "Somehow, the two-by-fours he purchased have been misplaced." The POW scratched his head, as if genuinely puzzled. "I believe they will turn up later, where he least expects them."

"You hid them?"

The POW shrugged. "I could not say yes. I could not say no." He motioned to Fish. "Come. You must see the dog."

Fish followed him to the front corner of the yard where Liberty was being kept.

"We are both prisoners, she and I." He looked very sad, and very young, as he said those words.

Fish stuck out his hand. "I'm Fish."

"Erich."

They shook.

"Thank you for helping us." Fish knelt outside the pen, tossing the food he'd brought through the holes in the wires. Liberty got up heavily. She gobbled up the scraps, then flopped back down.

"I am thinking the pups come soon." Erich studied her, lips pressed together. "I grew up around many animals. On a farm. Tomorrow or the next day."

Fish gripped the wire fencing. "I have to get her out of there."

Erich nodded. "He is a bad man."

Fish glanced over at Erich. His eyes were as blue as Roy's. His smile as warm as Mo's. It was hard to think of him as an enemy. Maybe he had been. Maybe he still was, in some ways. But they were allies, too, over Liberty. "It's that darned padlock." He yanked on the gate, shaking it hard, for emphasis.

"Yah." Erich rubbed his hand through his hair. "I have even looked at his key ring."

Fish jerked his head to stare at Erich.

"But there is no padlock key there." He turned his hands palms up. "I do not know where he keeps it."

Fish felt his eyes water. He couldn't cry. Not in front of a complete stranger.

Erich stood next to him, staring intently into the pen. As he started to speak, they heard the rattle of Mr. LaVache's truck returning. He reached into his pocket, handed something to Fish. It was a carving of a dog.

Fish stared at it in wonder. It was Liberty in miniature perfection. He'd got her ears, her face, her shape, just right. "For me?"

"Inside each piece of wood waits its true self, yearning to be revealed by the carver." Erich turned away from Liberty's pen. "This is true for people, too. We do not know what lies within until we are prodded into action." He tapped Fish's shoulder, indicating that he should vamoose. Then he returned to the chicken coop where he'd been working. Picking up a brush, he calmly stroked bright red paint over the faded boards, as if he could not hear Mr. LaVache carrying on like a wounded bull.

Fish step-clomped as quickly as he could off Mr. LaVache's property. He stopped once he reached the road. "Erich!" he called.

Erich's head turned, slightly. Fish knew he'd heard. "Thank you!"

He put the carving in his pocket, and Erich's words in his head.

What was his true self?

He had no idea. But he sure hoped it could save a dog.

CHAPTER TWENTY-THREE

‖‖‖

The Plan

Erich had fifteen dollars folded neatly into his sock to get him started. He laughed to think of his English instructor praising his gift for language. "I can barely hear your accent," he had told Erich. The instructor had no idea how handy that lack of accent would be.

Erich had told no one of his scheme. Not the Professor. And certainly not Oskar. After all his planning, Erich had decided. Today was the day.

Bouncing along in the back of the truck, away from the camp, Erich was for once glad to be working for LaVache. And for that pair of coveralls the man kept in the back shed. Erich planned to slip them on to hide the white stenciled PW on his pants and shirt. As soon as he could, he would ditch the uniform. Perhaps in that canal they passed on the way to LaVache's place.

Timing was crucial. He had planned to make his escape shortly after arriving at the farm. If there was going to be a head count – and there hadn't been any lately – it would come at the end of the day, as the truck was loaded up for the return to the camp.

The military truck juddered to a halt in the dusty yard. LaVache held a burlap sack in his hands. He barked instructions at Sergeant Tucker and then disappeared inside his house.

Dread scorched Erich, worse than the sun. What was that sack for? As calmly as he could, he walked to the dog's pen. The mother was there, panting from the heat, calmly nursing pups. He'd been right! They had come soon. Looked to be five of them.

After a time, another man arrived. Unshaven, he reeked of tobacco and an unpleasant something else. He sauntered right over to the dog pen and inspected the puppies.

LaVache came outside to confer with him, still carrying the sack. "What do you think, Pie?"

The other man, Pie, shook his head. "Naw. Nothing good here."

"Shoot. And after all the trouble I went to." LaVache ran his hand over his mouth. "I've got grits cooking. You feel like some eggs? I'll take care of them puppies later." He tossed the sack over the wire.

Erich wrapped his hands around the back of his neck. He felt hopeless. As sick at heart as he had been the day they were captured. There was nothing he could do. He whispered soft comforts to the dog in German.

But there is no comfort for a mother who would be robbed of her babies.

CHAPTER TWENTY-FOUR

Diving in Headfirst

Mo had the radio on while she made their breakfast. "And now for this news from the Pacific..." intoned the announcer. Mo turned up the volume. "Fighting on Peleliu continues to be static as Marines are slowly pushing the enemy toward the north end of the island. About three-fourths of this island in the Palaus is now in our hands..." Fish chewed his cornflakes as quietly as possible to listen to the report.

"Seated with me today is Commander Powell of the US Navy, who is one of the very first eyewitnesses back from the Palaus. Commander —"

Mo clicked the radio off. "I can't stand to listen." She took a shaky sip of coffee. "Sorry, Fish. Sometimes it just gets to me."

"It's okay." Fish had been jittery, too, from the moment he first opened his eyes that morning. A change of topic would do them both good. "How's the studying going?"

"Mr. Haddock is not making it easy for me, that's for sure." Mo managed a small smile. "But he actually said 'fine' to my drawings yesterday. His *fine* is someone else's *fabulous*."

"Pop's going to be so proud of you when he finds out." Fish poked at the last of the flakes in his bowl. Mo had talked Mr. Haddock into teaching her how to make engineering drawings. She'd got it in her head to go to college. After the war. She hadn't even told Pop yet.

"And of you, too," she said.

"Me?" Fish shook his head. "Why?"

"Too many reasons to name." Mo finished her coffee and stood up. "You're a chip off the old block." She washed her breakfast dishes, then untied the apron she'd been wearing over her work clothes.

"You should've seen all the gizmos he worked on when I was a kid."

"Pop?" Fish picked up his breakfast dishes.

"Pop." Mo pinned her hat on. "And he was always a sucker for a stray dog. Just like someone else I know. Mr. Disappearing Scraps from the Icebox."

Fish nearly dropped his cereal bowl. "I didn't think you'd notice."

Mo opened her compact to apply her lipstick. "At least someone appreciates my cooking. Even if that someone gets around on four legs." She blotted her lips on a tissue, threw it in the trash, and snapped her compact shut. "You better skedaddle to school. I'll see you tonight."

Fish washed out his breakfast bowl and set it on a tea towel to dry, thinking about Pop. It was like Mo had one father, and he had another. Pop with Mom. Pop after Mom. The Pop he knew only grumbled about the mess Fish made with his inventions. And he'd never once offered to let Fish get a dog. Fish didn't even know that Pop liked them. He would've liked Liberty, if he'd had the chance to meet her. If Fish had been more careful, Liberty would still be his.

As Fish tied his shoes, he remembered that it was current events day. Luckily, yesterday's newspaper was on top of the garbage. He gingerly lifted it out, brushed off some coffee grounds, and grabbed a pair of scissors. Maybe there was something about the battle on that island. What was it? Peleliu? The kitchen clock tick-tick-ticked as he scanned the front page. There! In the fourth column. The article carried over to the next section. He clipped both selections and read them as fast as he could. He grabbed his books, checking the time. He'd be tardy if he didn't get a move on. Which meant there wouldn't be time to check on Liberty on his way to school.

Unless he rode his bike.

He peglegged down the back steps and grabbed the Schwinn, propelling himself out of the yard, down the street, toward Mr. LaVache's. The Army truck was already there, parked on the opposite side of the street from Mr. LaVache's old beater. Fish wobbled into a sharp turn, making for the next corner, planning to ride down the road at the back. He ditched the bike, and looked for Erich.

Erich spotted him, easing away from the work detail to meet up with Fish behind the far chicken coop.

"The puppies were born, sometime yesterday," Erich said.

"It must've been after I left!" Fish couldn't believe he'd missed that. "Is she okay?"

"From what I can tell, yes." Erich cleared his throat. "He spoke with a friend. A friend with a strange name."

"Pie," Fish filled in. "Pie DuFour. He thinks he's a dog expert. Can tell if the pups are worth —" The words got stuck. Fish couldn't say them. "What do they look like to you?"

Erich shrugged. "Little butterballs. Two marked like Mama. Three all red."

"Do they look like hunters?"

"They are brand-new. Helpless as chicks. More helpless." Erich shook his head.

"I have to find out what Pie says." Fish started forward.

Erich held him back. He couldn't bear to tell this boy what he had heard. But he must. "This man says the puppies are no good for hunting."

Fish's stomach cramped, threatening to upchuck cornflakes right there. "Is he really going to do it?" When Erich didn't answer, Fish thought perhaps he didn't understand the question. "Is he . . . taking the puppies?"

Erich stared at the toes of his boots. "I saw him with a large cloth sack."

At that moment, two men emerged from Mr. LaVache's house. Pie climbed in his truck and drove away. Mr. LaVache walked over to the dog pen, grabbed a large burlap sack off the fencing, whistling as if what he had planned was a picnic in the park.

"It's not going to happen." Even though his legs felt as limp as steamed okra, Fish began to move. Away from Erich, away from the chicken coop, away from the horrible scene. "Keep an eye on Liberty!" he shouted. He threw himself on the bike and slid and skidded his way to the front of the street. At that moment, Mr. LaVache tossed a burlap sack into the bed of his truck. A wiggling burlap sack. He hopped into the truck's cab and the engine rattled to life.

Fish pedaled with all of his might after that old junker. It clunked along, stalling out at every other stop sign, but Fish never stopped moving. He stayed with the truck all the way to the New Basin Canal. At a low spot in the road, Mr. LaVache parked the truck and stepped out. Hitching up his pants, he strolled around to the rear of the truck. He hefted the burlap sack, holding it away from him as if it were filled with manure, not Liberty's puppies.

The front wheel of his bike slipped on the gravel and Fish went down. A sharp rock jabbed into his lower back and the bike chain chewed up his pant leg. He scrabbled and pushed, wrestling the bike off him as if it were an octopus. He got to his feet just as Mr. LaVache swung his arm back. It snapped forward. He let go.

The bag landed with a splash.

Mr. LaVache climbed back in his truck.

Fish ran to the edge of the canal. He could see the bag barely afloat. He didn't stop to think. He dived in.

It was cold. Colder than a snowball. He gasped, sucking in the dark water slick with boat fuel and oil and who knew what else. He bobbed up, coughing and gagging, eyes stinging from the filthy water. The bag! Where was it?

Nurse Meg's voice filled his head. "You're quite the fish. A very strong swimmer." This was no therapy pool, but Fish kicked his legs — both of them — and stroked at the water with all his might.

He threw his arms in front of him, reaching out, reaching for the bag that was sinking lower and lower. His fingers brushed against something soggy and rough. Burlap. He grabbed for it, and missed, misjudging how far away it was. His lungs felt like they were going to explode. The bag drifted lower. He willed his legs to kick and he torpedoed closer, snagged the bag by the very edge. He shot up, up to the slimy surface of the canal, yanking the bag to safety, holding it above his head.

Water or tears or both ran down his face. He flipped the bag so it was on his back as he kicked and pulled and kicked and pulled to the canal's edge. When his fingers touched concrete, he grabbed hold, dragging himself and his parcel up and over the lip, falling face-first on the shoulder. Gravel scraped his knees as he knelt, heaving, forcing the tainted water out of his gut.

He gathered himself together and untied the sack. Inside, four wet pups coughed and trembled and mewled. The fifth lay deathly still. Fish lifted it out, tenderly rubbing its round belly. A tiny sound — baby bird–like — escaped from its mouth and then it moved, too. "You'll be okay. I'm going to take care of you. You'll be okay." He repeated the words over and over, trying to convince himself as much as the puppies.

The only way he could figure out how to get them home was to keep them in the sack. He balanced it on his lap as he rode, shivering and wet. Halfway there, he realized he needed help. He couldn't take care of the puppies and rescue Liberty, too. And they needed their mother. Pronto.

Miss Zona's face was pure surprise when she opened the door to Fish's knock. But she quickly took over. "I'll get them warm. But they need their mama," she said.

"I know. I'm going after her."

Miss Zona dumped sewing scraps out of a large basket and placed the puppies, one at a time, inside. "That man's pure misery. I know his wife left him when their boy passed, but that's no excuse for his meanness." She lifted the basket in her arms. "You be careful, Fish."

"I will." Fish had no idea what his next step would be, besides changing out of his wet clothes.

He ran home and threw on a dry shirt and pants. Then he tore out the front door.

There, ready to knock, was the telegram delivery boy.

CHAPTER TWENTY-FIVE

Bad News Times Two

If Fish hadn't already emptied his stomach at the canal, he might have again.

"Miss Mo Elliott?" The delivery boy shifted to look over Fish's head into the house. "Is she here?"

"No." Fish couldn't hold his hand steady. "I'll take it."

"You eighteen?" the boy asked. "Can't hand it over unless you're eighteen. That's the rules."

"Can you leave it with my neighbor, then?" Fish pointed to Miss Zona's. "She's way older than that."

"Nope." The kid tapped the envelope on his hand. "Can you telephone Miss Elliott?"

Fish was tempted to snatch the telegram from the kid's hand. Memories of seeing Mrs. DeSoto that day flooded his thoughts. "Wait here."

He dashed inside and dialed the phone, so shaky

he missed the hole on the first turn of the dial. At the sound of Mo's voice, all he managed was a croak.

"Hello?" Mo paused. "Is someone there?"

Fish could almost see her on the other end, ready to hang up.

"Mo." He forced her name out.

"Fish?" Her voice dipped. "What's wrong? Are you calling from school?"

School seemed so far away that it almost sounded like a foreign word to Fish. He'd completely forgotten that was where he was supposed be. "No. No. Uh. Mo, you better come home." He didn't know how much to say.

"What's going on?"

He had to practice the word in his mind before he could spit it out. "Telegram."

"I'm on my way." The receiver clunked in his ear.

Fish grabbed his shoes as he returned to the front porch. He sat on the glider; it took two tries to get the laces tied. Maybe it wasn't bad news. Then he could ride over to Mr. LaVache's the second Mo got home. Time was running out. Unless he stopped somewhere on the way home, Mr. LaVache had to be back from the canal already.

"She'll be here soon," Fish told the delivery boy. He noticed trickles of sweat creeping down from under the kid's hat, along each side of his face. "You want something to drink?"

"That'd be nice." The kid leaned against the porch rail.

Fish brought him a Dr. Nut soda. The kid took a long, deep drink.

"This was my brother's job." He exhaled. "Then he enlisted and I took over." The kid held the bottle to his lips. "I hate it. Nothing but bad news." He shot a glance at Fish. "Sorry. I shouldn't have said that."

"It's okay." Fish couldn't keep his legs still as he sat on the glider. They swung back and forth, back and forth, back and forth. Staring down the street didn't seem to make Mo come faster. The delivery boy didn't say anything else. Just sipped at his soda.

Fish had been watching for Mo to come from the streetcar stop, but now a sedan bumped up to the curb, the passenger door flew open before the car even came to a stop, and Mo flew out, too. She ran up to Fish, grabbing his hand. Mr. Haddock slid out of the car, but stayed down on the banquette.

"Mo Elliott?" The delivery boy held out the envelope when Mo nodded. "Thanks for the drink," he said to Fish. Then he leaped down the stairs to his bike, and rode away.

Mo took a seat on the glider. She tore open the envelope, skimming across the words. She sucked in a breath, as if it hurt to breathe. "It's Roy." She cleared her throat. "He was, was injured at Peleliu." Her hands, still holding the telegram, fell to her lap. Fish sat next to her, unsure of what to do. Mr. Haddock made his way up the steps.

"Can I be of assistance?" He turned his fedora around in his hands.

Mo shook her head. "Oh, wait. Will you tell Mr. Higgins I won't be in the rest of the day?" Her voice was tight, controlled.

"Sure thing." Mr. Haddock put his hat back on. "Take tomorrow off if you need to."

From the glider, Fish and Mo watched Mr. Haddock get in his sedan and drive off. Fish's insides were twisted like snarled shoelaces. He knew he should stay with Mo, but the longer he sat here, the less chance he had of saving Liberty. Saving her pups.

Mo had been staring off into space. She blinked, wiped her eyes, and focused on Fish. "Why aren't you in school?" she asked. "And why is your hair all wet?"

Fish wasn't sure how she'd react. But he told her what had happened.

"You jumped in the canal?" Her hand went to her mouth. "Oh my gosh, Fish. What if something had happened to you?" She crumpled the telegram in her lap. "It's too much. Too much."

"Those puppies need their mom," he said. "Which means I have to save Liberty."

"No." Mo slapped her hand against her leg. "It's crazy. You can't."

Fish stood up, remembering Mr. Higgins's words. "The only thing I can't do is give up." Something had happened to him in the canal. Miss Zona once tried to talk him into getting baptized. "The water washes the old self away," she'd said. That's how he felt since rescuing the pups. Like a new Fish had emerged from that water. As if his true self had worked its way out of the wood, like Erich's carvings. And this Fish wasn't going to let Liberty or her puppies down.

Fish turned away from his sister.

Mo stood, too. "Then I'm coming with you."

Fish shook his head. "Only room for one on my bike. One person, anyway."

"All right, then. I'll go help Miss Zona with the puppies." Mo's smile was watery. "You go get your dog."

Fish pedaled for all he was worth. He didn't even ride to the back of Mr. LaVache's this time. He barreled into the front yard. Right up to Liberty's pen.

It was empty.

CHAPTER TWENTY-SIX

Sleight of Hand

Their work finished, Sergeant Tucker ordered the prisoners into the truck for the return to camp. Erich dawdled. He had to see what happened. He'd postponed his escape because of the dog. The boy. So much like Friedrich, ready to tilt at windmills. This sad world needed more like them. Such good hearts would find the way to a better future. Erich ignored Sergeant Tucker's second instruction to finish up. He put away his tools one by one.

As if on cue, the boy barreled down the road, left leg pumping the pedals, stiff right leg acting as ballast. His hair was soaking wet. But his face told the important part of the story. He had saved the puppies. And now he was back to save the dog. He careened from the street, straight for the pen. He nearly crashed into it, he was that out of control.

"Liberty!" Fish screamed the word. He threw the bike down, gripping the mesh around the pen, shaking it in frustration. His white face swung toward Erich, exhaustion mixed with disbelief. "Where is she?" Sweat or perhaps tears left muddy tracks on his cheeks.

Erich glanced away at a noise. LaVache's truck. Time was running out. He put his finger to his lips, motioned Fish close to the Army truck. From inside, one of the other prisoners handed out a pair of coveralls rolled into a bundle. A large bundle that sprouted a tail.

Erich so wished he could have taken a photograph of the boy's face. The look of astonishment. Admiration. Gratitude.

The boy reached out for the coveralls.

Erich gave it a final pat. "She is in good hands now, yes?"

The boy was apparently too overwhelmed to speak. He merely nodded.

"You must go. Hurry." Erich picked up the bike and put it in the truck. "We will drop this off on the next corner. You can get it later."

The boy rearranged the bundle in his arms and began to run. It was stiff-legged, but it was a run. Erich smiled. The boy would be all right.

So would the dog.

He saluted them as they made their way to freedom.

CHAPTER TWENTY-SEVEN

Pleased to Meet You, Mr. President

Fish sat on the floor, Liberty next to him, with the puppies tumbling around in his lap while Mo read the letter from Roy. *"Don't worry about me. I'm healing up just fine,"* he wrote. *"Should be able to get back to the ship in another week. This will probably get censored, but if I were a betting man, I'd bet that we'll all be together again in the new year. Now I have a favor. Could you pass the enclosed on to Captain McDerby? I don't mind if you read it. In fact, please do."* Mo paused, pulled another sheet of paper out of the envelope and began to read:

Dear Captain McDerby,
Since coming back from real action, we certainly found out and appreciate what you taught us and which we were able to put to good use. The landings made on the beaches went exactly as planned, the way you taught us. I will confess that I didn't fully appreciate your being so strict and demanding,

but now that I've been in combat, I understand what you were trying to do. It's hardly the time to learn to beach a boat when the enemy is blasting you with all they've got. If it hadn't been for your high standards, there would have been far more casualties in the fighting. Please use this letter, in your own words of course, to help other students who might feel as I once did. I am eternally grateful to you.

Roy Weathers

"Are you going to give that to Captain McDerby?" Fish asked.

"You bet. With a thank-you note of my own." Mo slipped the letter back into the envelope. "Maybe I'll even bake him some cookies."

"Or maybe ask Miss Zona to bake some?"

Mo put her hands on her hips. "Are you saying I can't bake?" Then she laughed. "Good idea. I'll ask Miss Zona."

Fish rolled onto the floor, and the puppies romped over and around him, chasing one another. "Are you sure I can't keep one? You said Pop likes dogs." A pup nipped at him with tiny needle-sharp teeth. He gently pushed her away. "Easy there, tiger."

"Pop might like one dog," Mo said. "Not a pack of them." She bent over and picked up the runt. "They're so adorable. You won't have any trouble finding homes for them."

As if she knew what they were talking about, Liberty moved her head and placed it on Fish's leg, studying him with her brown eyes. "Don't worry, girl." He stroked her muzzle. "I'll make sure they get the best homes ever." Mr. Haddock had asked after one of the pups; so had the Beasley sisters. And Fish had an idea or two of his own about good families for the rest.

"You'll never guess." Mo started for the kitchen. "But I happen to know that Mr. Higgins is hosting a very special guest next month. A special guest whose initials are FDR." She winked.

"Yeah. I remember. For a tour of the plant."

"Well, Mr. Higgins thought you might like to meet him."

Fish sat back. "You're joking, right?"

"Mr. Higgins doesn't joke about things like this."

To meet Franklin Delano Roosevelt! "That'd be swell."

Fish disregarded Mo's wardrobe advice. This time he was comfortable in his aloha shirt, despite the heat in the plant. He fidgeted as he waited for the president's entourage. The first person he saw was Mr. Higgins sitting in the backseat of a touring car, waving as if he was running for office. Next to him was a tall man, sitting very erect, decked out in a dark suit topped with a polka-dotted bow tie and rimless glasses. Dark circles underscored his bright eyes; his face looked weary and worn out but not those eyes. They sparkled like a kid's.

The car eased to a stop and Mo nudged Fish forward.

"Mr. President," Mr. Higgins said, "I'd like you to meet the future. Mr. Michael Elliott."

As he'd practiced with Mo, Fish stood up straight, step-clomping his way to the side of the car. "I am honored to meet you, Mr. President." Fish got the words out without one stumble.

President Roosevelt smiled. "I would say the pleasure is all mine, young man. From what Mr. Higgins tells me, the future is in good hands if you're part of it."

Fish hadn't expected the president to speak to him. He hesitated before remembering the other line he'd practiced. "You're my hero, sir." He patted his leg. "I'm trying not to let this stop me, either."

"Men are not prisoners of their fates, but only prisoners of their own minds." The president nodded. "I think you will find, as I have, that little obstacles like these" — he patted his own legs — "make us stronger." He leaned toward Fish. "You should come to Warm Springs sometime."

There was something so friendly and familiar about this man that Fish blurted out something that he hadn't rehearsed. "You wouldn't like a friend for Fala, would you, sir? I have puppies who need homes."

Mr. Higgins frowned, but the president threw back his head and laughed. It was a strong laugh. A genuine laugh. "That is the best offer I've had in ages," he answered. "But Fala's used to running things on Pennsylvania Avenue. Don't think it'd be fair to the pup. But I do appreciate your asking."

"There are some employees waiting with a special message for you in the assembly room, Mr. President." Mr. Higgins signaled the driver to pull away.

"Nice to meet you, Michael!" The president tipped his hat. "And good luck! Higgins here better watch out — you might be giving him a run for his money one day."

Mo placed her hand on Fish's shoulder, giving it a squeeze. Together they watched the car drive off to the City Park Plant.

Fish looked up at his sister. "Wait till I tell Pop about this!"

CHAPTER TWENTY-EIGHT

A Visitor

"Berger!" Sergeant Tucker hollered out his name. "Visitor."

Erich sat up in his bunk, puzzled.

"Get the lead out." Tucker tossed Erich his boots.

This wasn't like Tucker. Something was up. But Erich followed him anyway, past the mess hall with its sign announcing TURKEY DINNER FOR THANKSGIVING and on across the grounds.

It was the boy, Fish, carrying a cardboard box. With his skinny little friend.

"The sergeant said it was okay," Fish said.

A wet black nose poked out.

"It's a girl," said the boy. "For you."

Erich held the box as if it contained Mutti's best china. He glanced at Tucker.

"I don't see anything," the sergeant said. "Besides, Barracks Ten has two dogs and a cat." He reached in and scratched the pup behind the ears. "Guess we better start stocking Milk-Bones in the canteen."

Two bright eyes met Erich's. For the first time in a long time, he was aware of his heart. Beating like a real human being's.

He set the box down and lifted the pup to his face. Her hind end waggled with pure joy.

"What are you going to name her?" the girl asked.

"Hoffen." Erich held the pup close. She nibbled at his chin with her needly puppy teeth. "She is Hope."

CHAPTER TWENTY-NINE

Just Like Any Boy

Fish carried the Waldorf salad over to Miss Zona's. Mo carried the pie. Her first ever. The crust was only a little burnt. "We'll whip some extra cream to cover that up," Mo said. Liberty trotted along at their heels; she'd been invited to Thanksgiving dinner, too.

Olympia threw open the front door before they'd reached the bottom step. "Grandmamma says I was about to wear a hole through the window glass watching for you." A pudgy bundle of puppy tumbled out onto the porch. Liberty loped up the steps, sniffing her daughter.

Mo handed the pie off to Olympia, then scooped up the puppy. "How is little Miss Delta today?"

"Smart as a whip." Olympia beamed. "Pretty near house-trained, too."

"Not quite," Miss Zona's voice boomed from the back of the house.

Olympia grinned. "Come on, Fish. You can help me fill the celery sticks with cream cheese."

Fish step-clomped through the front room and the commotion of Miss Zona's extended family, to follow Olympia back to the kitchen, Liberty at his heels. Olympia set the pie down and then she and one of her aunts showed him how to spread the cheese down the hollow in the celery stalks. Fish nibbled at a piece. Not bad.

Later, they crowded around Miss Zona's rickety table out in the yard, holding hands while she prayed the blessing. Next year, maybe Pop and Roy would be at the table, too. And after dinner, Pop could organize a football game, with Roy and Olympia's uncles and boy cousins. And maybe Fish would join in like any normal boy, running for a pass, in his own higgledy-piggledy way.

With Liberty running at his side.

AUTHOR'S NOTE

I have spent a lot of time reading and writing about World War II. As with most of life, there is always something new to learn. For example, though I've watched the movie *The Longest Day* nine million times (it's my husband's favorite), I had no idea there was a story behind the boats that transported soldiers to the beaches at Normandy. But when I paid a visit to the National WWII Museum in New Orleans, I learned all about the bigger-than-life Andrew Jackson Higgins, whose boats, according to General Eisenhower, won the war for us.

So when I was asked to write a companion book to *Duke* and *Dash*, I knew I wanted to set it in New Orleans. Imagine my surprise when research also revealed a prisoner of war camp, Camp Plauche, that housed thousands of German soldiers, right in New Orleans. And, in fact, not all that far from one of Mr. Higgins's plants!

I so wanted to tie these two story elements together, but it took me a long time to figure out how to do it, so long that I nearly gave up. Once Erich came to life on the page, I knew he had to be part of Fish's story, despite the number of false starts in finding my way.

Though Mr. Higgins was ahead of his time in hiring women, minorities, and even the differently abled (one welder who worked for him had no arms!), he was a man of his times in that his white and black employees worked on different lines. An African American who wanted a job at Higgins Industries had to enter the building through the basement, while a white prospective employee went in through the main door. As the book reflects, throughout New Orleans, there were separate restrooms, movie theaters, water fountains, even COLORED ONLY streetcars. Black and white children attended different schools and some public parks were off-limits to children of color. And yet, neighborhoods were not necessarily segregated.

Whites and blacks might live next door to one another, as did Fish and Olympia.

My editor asked me if these two characters would really have had the chance to be friends in 1944, given the racial attitudes of the time. As someone who moved around a lot as a kid, I believe it was possible. I was often befriended by kids simply because we were neighbors; they might completely ignore me at school (I was pretty nerdy), but we would still play kick the can together of an evening. People are complicated; individuals rarely fit into neat boxes. And I suspect there were exceptions to every "rule," even during those harsh times of the Jim Crow South. I've noticed that big changes often start small: In the 1940s, there may well have been people like Fish and Olympia whose childhood friendships led them to the work of the sixties, breaking down barriers to build bridges of the heart, work which, sadly, is still needed today.

ACKNOWLEDGMENTS

It takes a team to make a book, and the team for this one was even bigger than usual. I had tremendous help from Gemma Birnbaum, Digital Education Coordinator, and Kimberly Guise, Curator/Content Specialist, both at the National WWII Museum in New Orleans; Erin Kinchen, Reading Room, Louisiana State Museum Historical Center; Greg Lambousy, Director of Collections, Louisiana State Museum; and Robert Ticknor, Reference Assistant, the Historic New Orleans Collection, Williams Research Center. I am especially grateful to my eyes and ears in New Orleans, Dr. Sarah Borealis. If you want to know more about Andrew Jackson Higgins, read *Andrew Jackson Higgins and the Boats That Won World War II*, by Jerry E. Strahan. The letter that Roy writes to Captain McDerby was actually written by Navy Coxswain Edward A. Weathers and is found in a more complete form in Mr. Strahan's biography. I am so thankful to everyone who lit a candle to help me find my way through wartime New Orleans. Any errors in this book are mine alone.

I've got to give a shout-out to Mr. T. J. Shay's fifth graders who helped to name Liberty and her pups. And thanks to my Butterfly Sisters — Susan Hill Long, Barbara O'Connor, and Augusta Scattergood — for laughs, encouragement, and well-placed swift kicks. As always, this book actually has a plot courtesy of the insight of Mary Nethery.

I won the lottery when I was matched up with editor Lisa Sandell; you wouldn't be holding this book if not for her guidance, and for the efforts of Jennifer Abbots, Julie Amitie, Bess Braswell, Michelle Campbell, Caitlin Friedman, Antonio Gonzalez, Emily Heddleson, Christine Reedy, Lizette Serrano, Whitney Steller, Tracy van Straaten, Rebekah Wallin, and the entire sales team; to Lori Benton, Ellie Berger, David Levithan, and Dick Robinson;

Alan Boyko, Jana Haussman, Janet Speakman, Robin Hoffman, and the whole Book Fair crew. Thanks to everyone at Scholastic for caring so much about getting books into kids' hands.

I am ever grateful to Jenni Holm for the matchmaking job between me and Jill Grinberg Literary Management: Jill, Cheryl Pientka, Katelyn Detwiler, and Denise St. Pierre, you are the best!

Love and gratitude to my family: Neil, thanks for listening to me whine and for taking care of Winston while I'm off doing research; thank you, Quinn, Matt, Tyler, and Nicole for giving me my favorite job ever: Grandma. And smooches to Eli, Esme, and Audrey, who love stories as much as I do.

When WWII comes to the homefront, these kids and their dogs will have to be brave...

The Dogs of World War II Novels
By Newbery Honor Author Kirby Larson